# The Thrilling Life of
# Pauline
## de Lammermoor

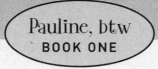

Pauline, btw
BOOK ONE

# The Thrilling Life of
# Pauline
# de Lammermoor

## EDEET RAVEL

RAINCOAST BOOKS

*Vancouver*

Raincoast Books gratefully acknowledges the ongoing support of the Canada Council for the Arts, the British Columbia Arts Council and the Government of Canada through the Book Publishing Industry Development Program (BPIDP).

Edited by Colin Thomas
Cover and interior design by Teresa Bubela

Library and Archives Canada Cataloguing in Publication

Ravel, Edeet, 1955-
   The thrilling life of Pauline de Lammermoor / Edeet Ravel.

ISBN-13: 978-1-55192-988-0
ISBN-10: 1-55192-988-0

I. Title.

PS8585.A8715T57 2007          jC813'.54          C2006-905236-0

Library of Congress Control Number: 2006937070

Raincoast Books                    *In the United States:*
9050 Shaughnessy Street            Publishers Group West
Vancouver, British Columbia        1700 Fourth Street
Canada V6P 6E5                     Berkeley, California
www.raincoast.com                  94710

Raincoast Books is committed to protecting the environment and to the responsible use of natural resources. We are working with suppliers and printers to phase out our use of paper produced from ancient forests. This book is printed with vegetable-based inks on 100% ancient-forest-free paper (40% post-consumer recycled), processed chlorine- and acid-free. For further information, visit our website at www.raincoast.com/publishing.

Printed in Canada by Webcom.

10 9 8 7 6 5 4 3 2 1

for Lucy (14) and Casie (16)
two inspiring girls
and, as always, for Larissa (19)

1

School is absolutely, definitely, incontestably OVER. For the summer, anyway.

And I, Pauline Carelli-Bloom, aged nearly 14, am going to spend the summer writing my very first novel.

I used to think I wanted to be an artist like my dad, who gets to paint all day in his studio upstairs, when he's not teaching art in elementary and high school. Then I changed my mind and decided I was going to be a pianist and wear long flowing gowns as I played on a massive grand piano to an awestruck audience. But after three weeks of piano lessons, my parents begged me to quit.

All that is behind me, however. Because now I know exactly what fate has in store for me: I'm going to be a world-famous, bestselling novelist.

Don't worry, I'm not on my own here. I have expert advice at the tip of my fingers. As of this morning,

I am the proud owner of *You Too Can Write a Great Novel!* by Zane Burbank III.

I won this amazing book as a prize for a story I wrote, entitled "Janitor Jones, Spy Handler." It was about our very cool school janitor, Ernest Peterson Jones, and how he really works for the CIA and runs a spy ring, and the janitor job is just a cover. And how the radio he keeps on at all times is really sending him secret codes — in rap.

Actually, I was very surprised that I won. I was sure my classmate Augusta was going to win. Her story was called "Death Be Not Proud," and I have to admit it sounded very good. It was about war, I think, and also about her pet hamster, who escaped from his cage and was never seen again.

All this happened on the last day of school, which, let me repeat, was TODAY. First we had to sit through about seven thousand boring speeches saying how great Newton School is, including one by our teacher Ms. Nipuitz, alias the Viper. The Viper has this double personality so that when she's in front of everyone else, i.e., parents, principal, other teachers, she's like this sweet woman who wouldn't harm a fly, while when she's alone with her class, behind a closed door, she reveals her true reptilian, venomous, bloodthirsty self.

Anyhow, after the speeches, they called up everyone who was getting an award or prize or some sort of honourable mention, and there I was, daydreaming away, when my best and loyal friend Genevieve poked me in the ribs and whispered excitedly, "You won, Pauline! You won!" Genevieve gets hyper when anyone wins something. She's only calm when she's the one winning, which happens all the time because she's a fantastic figure skater and she's constantly getting medals in competitions.

I was flabbergasted, actually. Thanks to the Viper, this was my worst year ever, academically speaking. I wasn't alone, though. Practically everyone in the class had a low pass average. We even began to compete at a certain point, to see who got the meanest comments on their work. *This is fine if you want to spend your life sitting on the sidewalk waiting for donations* was usually a close runner-up to *If this is your level of literacy at this point, I blame the educational system.*

But they were definitely calling my name. My story about Janitor Jones had won Best Short Story and my prize was two books:

1. *You Too Can Write a Great Novel!*
2. *Roget's Thesaurus*. A thesaurus, as you may know, is a dictionary that gives you about a thousand synonyms

for every word, including foreign phrases in Latin and other exotic languages. It's going to come in very handy in my new career.

I'm quite looking forward to writing this novel. I liked working on "Janitor Jones, Spy Handler" because it gave me a chance to get my point of view across. In real life, not everyone is interested in a teenager's point of view, I've noticed.

Zane Burbank III, the author of *You Too Can Write a Great Novel!* says not to make chapters too long, and besides, my mom needs to check her e-mail so I have to go.

*The end.*

(I mean of the chapter, not the novel!)

According to Zane Burbank III, there are two basic rules you have to follow to write a Great Novel.

First:

WRITE ABOUT WHAT YOU KNOW BEST.

Just my luck! I was going to write a longer version of "Janitor Jones, Spy Handler," but Zane Burbank says that if you write a spy thriller, for example, you have to do some serious research about spies and government agencies and weapons and codes, not to mention (in my case) mops and cleaning equipment.

The only thing I know a lot about is my life. And that's not exactly a seat-gripping, death-defying, action-packed, heart-rending adventure story.

However, according to the second rule:

YOU CAN MAKE ANYTHING INTERESTING.

Which means, even my life. *But how?*

Easy, according to Mr. Burbank III. All I have to do is apply the Five Writing Techniques.

1.  *Use lots of dialogue*
2.  *Include many details*
3.  *Be honest: reveal hidden truths*
4.  *Use interesting words* (which is where my thesaurus is going to be useful)
5.  *Be prepared to work hard*

I think I can apply those techniques, though I have one question about #3. I mean, how can I reveal hidden truths if they're hidden?

Maybe Zane means secrets. Maybe he means I have to reveal *my* secrets. But I don't really have any huge or shocking secrets. I don't have an eating disorder, I don't see dead people, and I've never committed a crime — though I certainly *thought* of several crimes I'd like to commit when I was in the clutches of the Viper.

Still, I'll do my best. I don't think it'll be too hard, because I'm more like my mom, who says what's on her mind, than my dad, who's more your Silent Type.

Mom doesn't believe in holding back. If she has something she wants to say about what a hard day she had at work with her ex-con clients, or about how daughters should be more helpful around the house, she comes right out and says it.

Dad's completely different. He's a nice guy, but he tends to be reticent, unloquacious, indisposed to talk, laconic, and tells it not in Gath.

Not surprisingly, my parents are divorced.

I have to go, Mom's calling me to set the table for supper. I'll tell you all my *hidden truths* tomorrow.

Today I was going to reveal *hidden truths*, but Zane says I have to start off by *setting the scene*.

So today I will set the scene, which means giving some background information about myself. To begin with, I'll tell you who I am, where I live and who my friends are.

First my age, which is a touchy subject. It's not actually a hidden truth, because I tell everyone I meet the sad story of how, thanks to my irresponsible parents, I'm a year behind in school. I'm supposed to be going into grade eight, but I'm going into grade seven. The reason I'm one year behind is that I missed kindergarten. My parents decided to go on a six-month trip to Europe when I was five. They wanted to take me with them on the whole trip, but I kept embarrassing them in Paris. So they dumped me at my grandmother's in London and went off by themselves.

My grandmother was very kind, but she sent me to a program for intellectually challenged kids. She said it would "deepen my sense of equality with my fellow beings," and besides, the program was in a church basement right across the street from where she lived.

That wouldn't have been so bad in itself. I mean, those kids were nice, the church ladies were nice, and I had fun. But my grandmother told the church people that I was intellectually challenged too! And they believed her!

I didn't find that out until much later, but it explained a lot of things. I used to wonder why those two ladies were always so impressed by everything I did. "Drank that all by yourself, did you, now! Wonderful, Pauline!"

It's a miracle I didn't turn out dark and bitter, after that year. I'm a very forgiving person.

We don't have split classes in my school, so when I came back to Canada, I had to go into kindergarten, because I wasn't ready for grade one. The only thing I learned in the church basement was how to sing "Twinkle Twinkle Little Star." Mostly we went for walks and hung out in the playground.

On top of this misfortune, I'm tall for my age, so people often think I'm older than I really am.

They think I've been left behind *two* grades, not one, because everyone in my class is so much shorter than me. I was five foot eight and a half inches last time I checked. The only girl who's taller than me is Tina, my old enemy from daycare. She's on the boys' basketball team.

I always tell my teachers the reason I'm a year behind. This was a big mistake, however, in the case of the Viper, who immediately began calling on me for the hardest questions, because, as she put it, "At your age, a year should signify substantial intellectual development."

To return to *setting the scene*, apart from my height, my only other distinguishing features are my hair, which is purple and blue, and my long feet. I dyed my hair purple and blue as an experiment — I wanted to see how my parents would react. My dad said, "Those shades complement each other quite well," and Mom barely noticed. That's what happens when your father is an artist and your mother is a social worker. To Dad I'm a good colour combination and to Mom I'm no different from the women at the halfway house where she works, who are eager to experiment with their hair after enduring the limits placed on them in prison. Anyhow, one big advantage of purple and blue hair is that it distracts people from my long feet. I have a lot of trouble finding shoes that don't look dorky on me.

Now I'll tell you about my home. I live in Canada, in this small town called Ghent, which is named after a medieval abbot, Gilbert of Ghent. It only has one mall, though I must say it has at least twenty very good restaurants. It's about a two-and-a-half hour drive from Toronto. The house I grew up in is a hundred years old and quite large. It doesn't feel all that large, though, because Dad uses the entire upstairs for his art studio, so my bedroom is on the main floor.

The main floor has three big rooms and one small one. I'll draw it for you, because I always wonder what houses look like when I read a novel. First I imagine one house (mine, even though I know that's dumb) then I imagine another (Genevieve's or some other house I've been to) and it's kind of annoying for the house to keep changing. So I'll include a floor plan of the main floor of my house at the end of this novel.

As you can see from the floor plan, the big rooms are the kitchen, the living room, and my bedroom, which used to be a dining room. The small room is a den, which used to be Mom and Dad's bedroom before they got divorced and which is now filled with Mom's boxes, because Dad sleeps upstairs in his studio and Mom moved out. My parents have shared custody of me, which means I also live in Mom's place. I'll tell you more about her place another time.

I also have a very cool grey and white cat. Her name is Stormy Weather and she likes to squeeze in between people. So if you're sitting next to someone on the sofa, she'll immediately jump up and slide herself between the two of you. The squishier it is, the more she likes it.

That brings me to the last topic, which is my friends:

1. Genevieve. I already mentioned her. She's my best friend. She has a few freckles on her nose and brown hair and a friendly skinny face, and she's a fantastic figure skater — I already mentioned that too, but I'm reminding you in case you forgot. Genevieve has five brothers: Raymond (18), Leon (16), Mark (9), Daniel (5) and Matthew (infant). Mom says, "I don't know how Genevieve's mother does it. After you, I couldn't imagine having even *one* more baby." That makes me feel great, Mom.

2. Leila. Math and science whiz, born in India near the mountains (she showed us a picture). Her mom is a

dentist who is obsessed with flossing. Every time Leila's mom gives us a lift in their van, we get a long lecture on Flossing And Why It Will Prevent Your Teeth From Falling Out. Then she hands out little floss samples. Leila doesn't mind. She's too busy thinking about Kalan, the Canadian Idol. Leila is in love with Kalan, though "love" is too weak a word to describe her obsession. Her bedroom is a shrine to Kalan. The walls are covered with every picture ever taken of Kalan, and she can probably tell you how much he weighed when he was born and when each of his teeth grew in. She's planning to be a doctor and her biggest fantasy is that Kalan will have some mysterious health problem, like a strange humming in his ears, which only she will be able to cure. Naturally, he'll fall instantly in love with her.

3. Rachel. You have to be open-minded about Rachel, because she belongs to some religion where you're not allowed to watch TV or even listen to the radio. She lives with her grandmother and wears lumpy sweaters, and her blonde hair is always braided in a very old-fashioned, Anne of Green Gables sort of way. Still, there's something to be said for her lifestyle. For example, she has a weaving machine at home and she and her grandmother make dolls' clothes that they sell.

That's fairly cool. I wouldn't mind knowing how to weave. *Pauline Carelli-Bloom, novelist and weaver* has a nice ring to it.

4. Augusta. Every now and then Augusta P. Lemarre (alias the Queen) joins us. She's really popular and has a lot of other friends, but she likes that Genevieve does figure skating, that my dad's an artist, that Leila's a math and science whiz, and that Rachel knows how to weave on a real loom. Sometimes we get mad at her, but she has her good points. She has a good sense of humour and she's really generous with advice on fashion, boys and shopping — her three areas of expertise. She travels all over the world with her rich parents and Will Smith once kissed her on the cheek. Life is extremely not fair.

5. Yoshi. He's a boy. And that's all I have to say about him. He only comes over so he can get tips on painting from Dad. He wants to be an artist and a sports broadcaster. My friends think he's coming over to see me and that I have a secret crush on him. This is not true. I don't have a secret crush on anyone. I used to have a secret crush on Stanley, the leader of the Jewish Kids Club, but that was long, long ago.

I'm half-Jewish (on my mom's side) and half-Italian (my dad's side). Until I was twelve, my Jewish half was active every Sunday morning, when I met with a bunch of other kids at the lounge of Ghent's only synagogue. Stanley, our leader, was very cute, but he was much too old for me, so I kept my feelings to myself. Since then, I've been entirely crush-free. However, there's no point arguing with my friends. Once they get something into their heads, it's stuck there forever, like burrs on a stray dog.

I have to go, Mom's calling me. This time she wants me to decide on Summer Activities. "I'm not going to have you staring at the computer screen ten hours a day for two months," she announced. I tried to explain that I'm working on a novel, but she wasn't impressed.

I may not include my mom in the acknowledgements page of my novel. That's the page where you thank people who were helpful in your *uphill battle with your creative demons* (Zane).

My mom is going to have to be a little more supportive if she wants to be on that page!

## 4

Mom signed me up for three Summer Activities: dance, mask-making and swimming.

I tried to get out of swimming, but Mom declared resolutely, "Swimming is as important as math and reading."

"But I already passed Red," I moaned.

"Yes, you did. Which is why I enrolled you in Maroon." Then, all of a sudden, her tone changed completely. "Just give it a try, Pauline. I'm sure you won't be sorry."

My mom always starts off really strict then suddenly goes all mushy. I figured out the reason. You see, she's trying to do a good job as a parent, and she thinks doing a good job means being decisive and consistent.

Except that her personality isn't decisive and consistent at all. She's a scatterbrain really. She opens a drawer and can't remember what she's looking for.

She does a load of laundry and leaves it in the machine for three days before she remembers about it. By then all the clothes have a stinking, putrid, vomity and ignoble smell.

And she spends hours and hours lying on the sofa-bed, munching on organic corn chips and watching videos. I ask you, does this paint a picture a social worker would be happy to see? I hope we never get a surprise visit from one. Questions regarding my mother's suitability as a parent could easily arise, and I'm not sure Dad, locked away in his studio and immersed in his art, would fare much better.

When I pointed this out to my mom, her excuse was: "My job is stressful. I need to unwind."

I guess her job *is* stressful. She works with women who have come out of prison. My mom helps them learn how to readjust to society.

"The biggest problem is that as soon as they're out, they start dating unsuitable men," she once told me.

"What's an unsuitable man?" I asked.

"Oh, you know. Robbers, murderers."

But to get back to my Summer Activities, it turned out that I was the only person over the age of ten who signed up for dance, due to the fact that my mother is in denial about needing reading glasses and read "ages 8–17" instead of "ages 8–11" in the brochure. Can you imagine how humiliating it was to enter a room in the Community Centre wearing my jazz ballet outfit and find a bunch of little girls looking up at me? Luckily, they assumed I was the teacher. I mumbled something about being in the wrong room and escaped. My mom forgot to recharge her phone for a change, and she was running errands, so I couldn't reach her to tell her about the mistake. I had to wait an hour for her to pick me up. I waited in the cafeteria. Since it was Mom's mistake, I felt no guilt whatsoever about helping myself to an extremely well-made lasagna with french fries and a milkshake, which Mom had to pay for when she arrived. My meal cost her less than the dance class, however, so she came out ahead.

Mask-making, on the other hand, is not bad. Our teacher is Goth, and on the first day she handed out black T-shirts with a spooky white mask and spiralling eyes. That brings my total T-shirt collection to 72. I'm seriously into T-shirts.

It all began with a T-shirt that once belonged to Dad. I found it in his rag pile — he was going to use it to wipe his paintbrushes. That was my first T-shirt rescue, way back in first grade. It says SOLIDARITY WITH EL SALVADOR, and under that there's a fist in the air.

It also says FRENTE DEMOCRATICO REVOLUCIONARIO. You have to admit, this T-shirt is very cool.

But mostly I like T-shirts that have jokes on them. The last one I bought shows Barbie in front of this big house and new car. Underneath, it says DIVORCE BARBIE: COMES WITH ALL OF KEN'S STUFF.

Some of my T-shirts Mom won't let me wear, like YOU'RE JUST JEALOUS THAT THE VOICES TALK TO ME, because she says mental illness isn't funny. She can be pretty humourless.

Others are sort of random but I like them. I have a T-shirt with Buddha on it, and it says BUDDHA KNOWS BEST. I like that one because of the fantastic colours. My prettiest one is DO THE RIGHT THING: PROTECT YOUR PLANET, with these birds of paradise on it. My grandmother, the one who lives in London, sent me that one. She's into environment issues.

My Dad's favourite is the one that says CANADA: HOME OF THE TWENTY-HOUR CLOCK. That's from this TV show where a guy goes to the U.S. and tells people things about Canada, like that we have a 20-hour clock instead of 24, and they fall for it. It *is* pretty funny, but it's not really fair, because how are people in the U.S. supposed to know about Canada? We're never in the news. Besides, you only get to see the people who believe everything you tell them, and not the ones who laughed in the guy's face.

Canada also has people who are trusting, gullible, easy of belief and dupable. I speak from sad experience. One summer when Genevieve and I were six and seven (she was six, I was seven), her brother Raymond came rushing into her room and told us World War Three had broken out, and that we had to go hide in the tool shed out back until it was safe to come out.

Genevieve's parents were away for the day with Mark, who was just a toddler back then. He was having some problem with his spine so they had to take him to Toronto to see a specialist. And the reason Raymond told us this big lie was that he wanted to have a party and he didn't want us getting in the way or telling on him. He brought us crackers and juice while we huddled in the tool shed hugging each other and crying.

Readers, it doesn't pay to be trusting. It's better to be doubting, skeptical, distrustful and from Missouri.

I could tell you a lot more about my T-shirts and World War Three, but I'm going to make myself stop, because Zane says, *Digressions are fine, but keep them short.* Digress means: stray, go adrift, fly off at a tangent and alter one's course. Ms. Nipuitz used to complain about that. She always wrote on my essays:

*Stay on topic, Pauline.* She is *such* a boring person.

Btw, in case you want to see what this unfortunate person looks like, I've made a little drawing for you. I'm not an artist like my dad, but I did my best. Augusta has her own website, which she set up last week — her dad showed her how. She said I could have some space on it, so I'll post the drawing of Ms. Nipuitz (illustration 1) on her website, just in case you want to see it. I think I'll also draw me and Genevieve huddling in the shed (illustration 2). All you have to do is go to **www.AugustaPLemarre.com** and you'll see the drawings there. I have to admit I like illustrations. My mom has old copies of books by Jane Austen and Charles Dickens, and they have great drawings of men leaning on mantelpieces and children being exploited. Zane says one of the bestselling books of all time, a novel called *Trilby*, had an illustration practically on every page. According to Zane, that's probably one of the reasons it did so well. That was long ago, however. Today people just wait for the movie.

Now, I'm going to *introduce conflict.* Zane says I have to *introduce conflict early in the novel* and here I am, already on Chapter 4, with no conflict.

According to Zane, the conflict has to be *trenchant.* Trenchant means sharp, biting, piercing and intense.

He gives three examples of *trenchant conflict*:

1.  *People fighting or tricking each other*
2.  *Countries fighting or tricking each other*
3.  *A person at a crossroads trying to decide which path to take*

I don't know much about countries in conflict and I don't know anyone who is at a crossroads, but I do have some serious experience in the area of people fighting — the people being my parents before they divorced (a year and a half ago). It was a long conflict, so I'll tell you about it in the next chapter.

5

The *trenchant conflict* between my parents gives me a good chance to insert dialogue. Here's some sample dialogue from just before my parents divorced:

"You never help with the laundry! I have to do everything around here!" my mom would accuse.

"I do a lot of things. I buy the groceries. I look after the car," Dad would protest.

"Those are things you do *outside* the house. I'm talking about things *inside* the house. How come I'm the only one who tries to keep this place in some kind of order!"

"You do it because it bothers you when things aren't under perfect control."

"Oh, that's a good one!" Mom would respond. "You'd be happy if you had no clean underwear? You'd be happy if all your dishes had slime crawling all over them?!" By now she was raising a hue and cry, getting hot under the collar, hitting the ceiling, flipping her lid and running amok.

"You know, Barbara, I'm really tired of all this nagging and complaining," Dad said. He didn't yell, though. Instead, his voice was spiritless, tactless, ungentlemanlike and infelicitous. (Zane says not to use "said" too often, unless you have an adverb right after it, or a description of the way the person sounded.)

"You don't even try to communicate!" Mom continued to shout.

"I don't like being yelled at," Dad answered.

"I wouldn't yell if you ever *talked* to me!"

"I'm going upstairs now."

"Typical! Typical! Go! Go talk to your paintbrushes, they won't make any demands."

While lovely conversations like this were going on, I'd hum very loudly. Usually I'd hum "If You're Happy and You Know It." I like irony.

I kept dropping hints to my parents so they'd notice how much their arguments were bothering, exasperating and martyring me.

For example, at suppertime I'd say innocently, "Genevieve's really lucky. Her parents never fight. It's so peaceful at her place."

This went right over my parents' heads. Actually,

it wasn't exactly true. I mean it's true Genevieve's parents don't fight, but I wouldn't exactly describe her house as peaceful. There are five boys living in that house. Use your imagination.

Another time, when I was still in daycare, I suggested: "Why doesn't Jill come live here?" Jill was my daycare worker. "She's good at fixing fights. If me and Tina are fighting about the pink Cadillac, Jill says to take turns."

Of course, in the case of my parents it wasn't that they both wanted to use the washing machine at the same time. In their case, *neither* of them wanted to use it.

"She could live in the laundry room," I went on. "She could use the laundry to make a nice, soft bed. Then Stormy Weather wouldn't have to hide under the sofa when you fight" (illustration 3).

You'd think if a kid said something that pathetic, his or her parents would stop fighting immediately. But no such luck. Mom and Dad went right on fighting through daycare, first grade, second grade, third grade, and half of fourth grade. Genevieve was very supportive. Whenever I told her about a fight she'd say, "*ma pauvre*," which means "my poor thing" but sounds really sympathetic in French, which is what her father speaks at home.

During this whole time, one of my mom's favourite songs, which she sang while she loaded the washing machine, was:

*Frankie and Johnny were lovers*
*Oh Lordy how they could love*
*They said they'd be true to each other*
*As true as the stars above*
*He was her man, but he done her wrong.*

I guess Johnny didn't help with the laundry either (illustration 4).

Several times Mom said, "When you love your child, it's forever and ever. But love between adults, well ..."

"What about Cinderella and the prince?" I asked, pretending to be a bit stupid. "They lived happily ever after."

"Yeah, well, if you have a fairy godmother that changes everything, doesn't it?" she said in a grumpy, peevish and nihilistic voice.

Another pre-divorce favourite was this really depressing ballad. I should mention here that even though my mom now works at a halfway house, she once studied to be an opera singer. She quit opera, though, as it was too hard. When you sing opera you have to sing from your diagram (illustration 5).

Anyway, when I was a little kid, I thought the ballad was about an old drunk dog. That's the type of mistake you make when your parents are too busy fighting to explain things properly to you. It goes like this:

*Oh I'm drunk today, but then I'm seldom sober*
*A handsome Rover, from town to town*
*Oh but I am sick now, my days are over*
*Come all you young lads, and lay me down.*

Which is funny, coming from my mom, who can't even have chocolates that have rum in them. She's allergic to fermented things (the rum, not the chocolate). As for the "rover" part, I did eventually figure out that the song wasn't about a dog named Rover (that's the Mockingbird song, which is how I got mixed up in the first place) but about a man who roves, which means to move around a lot. But for some reason, whenever I think of that song, I still imagine this big old dog walking around in a stupor because he's accidentally lapped up someone's beer.

I don't want you to think I was like one of those

kids you see in posters about child abuse, with dark circles under their eyes and messy hair. Actually, my parents were very nice to me. They just weren't all that nice to each other.

My best memory from when we were all one family was this Blue Sky Festival we used to go to every summer, with tents and all these old, old hippies listening to even older hippies playing guitar. Everyone would be in a great mood remembering all their hippie days when they wore beads, and this guy Mark came around with fantastic brownies, which also reminded people of happy days in the past, though these brownies were "ordinary" (illustration 6).

I asked my parents whether they had ever tried the original hippie brownies, but they both pretended not to hear me. Guilt was written all over their faces.

There was a painting table at the festival and my mom tried to paint animals, but her animals looked like pieces of left-over pizza. "Picasso, eat your heart out!" she proclaimed. My dad painted silly faces for me. And I made a mess, but my parents said I was an excellent abstract artist. Then at night we all sang "Row row row your boat" in a fugue.

The Blue Sky Festival is the one thing I kind of miss.

I think that's it for this chapter. As far as dialogue goes, I managed to get in 18 speeches (20 if you count the songs). Plus I put in some details, and used quite a few interesting words (I love this thesaurus!). The only thing I didn't do is *reveal hidden truths*.

Okay, here's a *hidden truth*: I figured out that my parents felt seriously guilty about arguing and then about divorcing. And this was good in a way, because it was pretty easy to make them give in and do stuff for me, like buy me more T-shirts. All I had to do was look pathetic. It doesn't work any more, though. My mom's finally seen through my act. "Don't try that pitiful look on me," she says. I think Dad's seen through it too, though he's still fairly easy to convince, because of his personality.

It sure took them a long time to catch up with me, though (illustration 7).

## 6

In this chapter I'm going to tell you about the marriage counsellor my parents saw. I was ten at the time.

"Pauline, your father and I are going to see a marriage counsellor to help us with our problems," Mom announced one day. I was on the floor of the living room munching on delicious cheese-flavoured tortilla chips and watching an old *Friends* re-run. Why did she have to ruin such a perfect moment? Why couldn't she wait until I was doing geography homework or something? Just when Rachel and Ross are about to kiss for the first time, in the rain, that's when Mom comes down from Dad's studio upstairs, where he does his painting, and destroys my peace of mind.

"Is she going to get you to sit in a circle and sing 'If You're Happy and You Know It?'" I asked. I was only joking, of course. I knew that a marriage counsellor was different from a summer camp counsellor, unfortunately (illustration 8).

"No, she's going to help us solve our problems," Mom said in a hopeful voice.

"I told you *years* ago that you should let Jill move in here," I said grumpily. "Anyhow, how does the counsellor know about solving problems?"

"She's read books," my dad muttered. He had just come down for a cup of Cofmalt, this fish-like goo he's forced to drink since he quit coffee. He sounded a bit derisive.

"She has, as a matter of fact," my mom agreed, ignoring my dad's tone of voice. "She's read hundreds of books and besides, she's not involved, she's on the outside, so it's easier for her to see what's going on."

"What's her name?"

"Dr. Nickels."

That was a pretty good name for the counsellor, because she charged a lot of money for solving problems.

The reason my parents told me all this is that I had to go with them to see Dr. Nickels a couple of times.

Dr. Nickels was a disappointment from the start. She was tall and skinny and wore a lot of jewellery and had thick glasses, and she looked very confused herself.

We met in her office, which was more like a room in a house, with sofas and armchairs and a coffee table in the middle. She wasn't wearing her stethoscope.

"So, Pauline, how are you?" she asked, once we were all seated. My mom and dad sat on the sofa as if they were best friends, and I sat in this elegant, cosy armchair, like Alice at the Mad Hatter's tea party. Like Alice, I may also have been the only sane person present.

"Fine, thank you," I replied politely.

"I mean, how are you *really*?"

"Oh. You mean what problems do I have?"

"Do you have problems?"

"Yes," I asserted. "I do, actually." Suddenly, I decided to expose my parents totally. After all, that's what they brought me here for. Why be shy? "The problem is my parents."

"Oh?"

"They're very childish," I informed her. "They can't agree on anything. They can't compromise. All they do is argue argue argue argue argue argue argue argue argue argue argue argue argue." I guess I got a little carried away.

"That's a lot of arguing," Dr. Nickels nodded sympathetically.

"Yup!" I agreed.

"What do they argue about?"

"Well, my dad won't eat at home. He says it makes him nervous. And my mom once threw a whole dish of lasagna she'd made on the floor because he wouldn't eat it. And my dad called her Lady Macbeth."

My parents began to look uneasy, cheerless, bothered and haunted.

Dr. Nickels turned to my dad. "Want to talk about it, Mr. Carelli?"

"Well, you see, I grew up in a very large family, fourteen people at every meal, give or take twenty. Everyone argued. My uncles about politics, my aunts about business, my cousins about sports. And my cousins kept kicking my legs to get me mad, because I was the only quiet one there. So I tried to eat very fast and get away quickly."

"So now …" Dr. Nickels tried to look neutral.

"So now eating with people makes me nervous."

"Where do you eat?"

"At the mall."

"Barbara, have you tried going to the mall with your husband?" Dr. Nickels asked my mom.

"I can't eat at the mall!" Mom objected. "The pizza is made with rubber cheese, the french fries are fried in grease from 1982, the quiche looks like someone's stomach insides!"

"You don't like the mall food," Dr. Nickels said calmly.

"No."

"How about three times a week you go to the mall and Barbara brings her own food with her, and three times a week you eat at home, and once a week you toss a coin?" Dr. Nickels suggested.

My parents had no choice but to agree.

On the way home, my dad said he didn't understand why he couldn't just go on eating at the mall all the time. He said Dr. Nickels was incompetent. Incompetent means: unskilled, unaccomplished, inept and unendowed.

Dr. Nickels' solution worked for about a week. My dad ate at home on alternating days, but he was obviously doing it under duress. Finally, my mom snapped, "Oh, just forget it. Go to the mall if you miss it so much" (illustration 9).

I only went to the marriage counsellor one other time. This time we talked about Grandma.

"I don't understand what Barbara has against my mom," Dad said morosely.

"She's trying to run our lives!" Mom fumed.

"Okay," Dr. Nickels said patiently. "Everyone will get a chance to speak. Mr. Carelli, why don't you go first?"

"My mom's lonely," Dad said defensively. "Everyone's grown up and moved away, my father ran off when we were kids, and now the only person she has is Uncle Vittorio, who's confined to a wheelchair and thinks he's Gary Baldy." (Whoever that is!)

"Okay, Barbara, your turn."

"That woman *is* Gary Baldy."

"Is this another argument that you don't like hearing?" Dr. Nickels asked me.

"You can say that again," I grumbled.

"Want to talk about it?"

"Not really," I replied. It was too hard to explain to Dr. Nickels. I really love Grandma, but it's true that I'm not too crazy about her tidying up my sock and underwear drawer every time she comes over. I mean, socks and underwear are kind of personal, and besides, what's the point, they're going to get all messy again soon. But she's great, aside from that. She gives me chocolate-covered marzipan, one of my absolutely favourite foods in the world.

Actually, Grandma was part of the Last Big Fight my parents had, the one where they decided to divorce, but I'll tell you about that in the next chapter, because this one's getting too long.

I did really well with dialogue in this chapter. On the other hand, maybe that's why the chapter is too long. I'll try to make the next one shorter.

# 7

I haven't written for two weeks, because it's been too hot. We had a crazy heat wave, probably due to global warming. It was a zillion degrees even at night. So Genevieve and I spent almost every day at my dad's above-ground pool out back. Not the whole day, because Genevieve has to practise at the ring — or is it "rink"? I can never get that straight.

Believe it or not, Genevieve wakes up at 5 a.m. to go skating for two or three hours in the morning *plus* she goes back in the afternoon for another two hours. If I had that kind of schedule, you'd have to take me away on a stretcher.

Finally it cooled down a bit, and my mom suggested we go camping. She told me I could invite Genevieve and Leila. Leila was away at science camp for three weeks, but she's back now, full of information about why the moon is not the sun and why leaves turn red in the fall. She said it was fun. This proves that people are very, very different from one another.

So the three of us and Mom all went camping for the weekend. I guess it's not really camping if you just go a few miles from where you live, but the fact is we have these huge camping grounds not too far from Ghent. And once we were there, sitting in our tent in the middle of the forest, we felt about as far from home as we'd feel in the middle of the Amazon rainforest — if there's anything left of it, that is.

There was a beach at the campsite too, and a grill thing, which we lit with the help of the family in a tent nearby. We roasted tofu burgers (my mom's into health food) and ate them with seaweed chips, which were quite tasty, in fact, and organically grown baked beans from a can, which tasted like regular baked beans, luckily. For dessert we had coconut soya cookies. They were surprisingly delicious. And Leila brought an excellent rice pudding that her mother made. Her mother also sent little dental floss samples for all of us, as usual, but Leila just laughed when she pulled them out of her backpack. "My mom is so sad," she said kindly.

We were really stuffed, but I couldn't help noticing that the kids next to us were eating assorted unhealthy chocolate bars from the kiosk. Mom doesn't like me to eat junk food, but I whined until I finally wore her down, and she let me go to the kiosk and buy chocolate bars for me and Leila. Poor Genevieve, she isn't allowed to eat junk food, because she's on an athlete's diet. She had to settle for a bag of cashews. Leila's not allowed to eat chocolate bars either, because of cavities, but as she put it, "What my mom doesn't know won't hurt her." She didn't even floss.

Genevieve and Leila and I had our own tent. It was a very noisy tent. It kept flapping and swishing in the wind, and making very loud sounds, as if huge flying demons were crashing into it. On top of that, one side kept coming loose and tickling me (illustration 10).

I thought at first we wouldn't fall asleep in such a noisy tent, so I decided to entertain Genevieve and Leila by telling them all about my novel. But I guess they were really tired, because in spite of the racket all around us, they both fell asleep just as I was explaining the difference between *setting the scene* and *trenchant conflict*.

I tried to fall asleep too, but the flapping tent bothered me, so I went out to look for some heavy stones. I found just what I needed, holding down our neighbours' tent. I know it's wrong to steal, but those people had about a hundred stones, so I figured they wouldn't miss one or two. Besides, stones are free. How can you steal something that belongs to Nature?

With the three heavy stones, my side of the tent stayed put, and I fell into a deep, blissful sleep.

We only camped that one night. I wish we could have stayed longer, like maybe all month. But Genevieve is on a very strict schedule, and my mom has to work during the summer. Only teachers — like my dad, who teaches art — get the whole summer off, and he hates to go camping. You'd think an artist would like nature, but he says he doesn't see the attraction of offering oneself as a living sacrifice to ruthless, ravenous mosquitoes. Lighten up, Dad!

Oops! I've already written quite a few paragraphs and I still have no dialogue. That's okay, because I was going to tell you about the Last Big Fight, and there's lots of dialogue in that part. I should probably start a new chapter, though, for the Last Big Fight, because this one took up more space than I planned. It's not always possible to plan ahead. Zane says, "*Let your words flow freely.*"

## 8

The Last Big Fight was right on my birthday, January 4. I was turning twelve. By then, I was dividing my birthday celebration into two parts: Friends Party and Family Party. At a certain point, friends and family don't mix at all well.

I'd already had my Friends Party. Genevieve and Leila and Rachel and I stuffed ourselves at Rock-a-Pie and then we saw one of those romance movies that are totally random but you kind of like them anyhow, in a random sort of way. Rachel wasn't allowed to see the movie, but she came anyhow. The way she did it was by not telling her grandmother.

The Family Party was supposed to be at our place. Mom was planning to have it catered by Mrs. Singh, who lives three doors down from us. But Grandma really wanted to make dinner for us at her place. So Mom gave in, but it put her in a bad mood. As you can see, things were already getting off to a bad start.

I like Grandma's apartment. It smells minty, it's full of lace covers for everything, and there's chocolate-covered marzipan all over the place, in little glass bowls. If you've never had chocolate-covered marzipan, I strongly recommend it.

Grandma's kitchen is small, but somehow she manages to make these humongous meals with about a hundred courses. Well, not a hundred, but at least eight. She loves to cook, and her two other kids and her other grandchildren (my aunt and uncle and cousins) live in Montreal and don't come in that often. She has a whole bunch of other relatives, but a lot of them are really old, or else they moved away to New York and Italy and (in one case) to the Virgin Islands. If I lived in a place called the Virgin Islands I would very simply kill myself.

Another thing I like about visiting Grandma is that I get to hear stories about what a weird kid my dad was. It's quite interesting to hear about your parents behaving strangely when they were kids. It explains a lot of things about their later lives.

Dad isn't thrilled by these stories, but Mom's like me, she enjoys them, even if she doesn't show it. But if you know her the way I do, you can tell she's listening with interest, mental acquisitiveness, rapt attention and voyeurism.

You'd think Grandma would have run out of stories by now, but she's always coming up with new tidbits. Like how when Dad was six, he told the dentist he was his brother Angelo, so that if the dentist hurt him, it would actually be his brother who was feeling the pain. That's pretty weird, you have to agree. Also a bit mean. Why should his brother feel the pain?

Uncle Vittorio also lives at Grandma's. I'm not sure whose uncle he is. He's pretty old, and he had a stroke so now he's in a wheelchair. Grandma doesn't want him to go to a home so she looks after him herself. It can't be easy. Uncle Vittorio is very nice, but he doesn't really know where he is or who he is (illustration 11).

Anyhow, as I was saying, Mom was in a bad mood from the start of this dinner. Matters were not helped by the constant "tips" my grandma kept giving Mom on how to get pots really clean, what to do if your soup is too salty (add a raw potato), how to get stains off a tablecloth, how to make lasagna that isn't all soggy, and how to take better care of me. "She is too young to be alone in the house. What if a thief comes?"

"Thanks for the advice," Mom said bitterly. She was ready to strangle Grandma by then. "If Pauline ends up selling drugs on the street, I'll know why."

Luckily, just then Uncle Vittorio said, "I saved a slave from drowning."

It wasn't until dessert that Grandma made the fatal announcement. She said that my birthday present was very special this year. Usually she gets me sweaters, but this year she said she wanted to do something really wonderful because, as she put it, "Now you are a woman."

That statement, which was delivered in a very loud voice, was almost as embarrassing as living on the Virgin Islands. But the commotion that followed her announcement made me forget about being embarrassed. Her present was four tickets to Florida, including Disney World, for her and me and Mom and Dad. "If you can't go because of work, Barbara, we can go without you," she added generously.

Mom proclaimed, "A family vacation has to be discussed with everyone before you go ahead and plan it."

Dad said in a low voice, "Thank you, Mom, that's very kind of you. It sounds like a lot of fun." He was lying. He hates planes, he hates being a tourist, and I think he'd rather be kidnapped by guerrillas in a South American country than go to Disney World. He doesn't like crowds.

Mom repeated, "We have to discuss it. Are the tickets refundable, by any chance?"

"Ah, no, no," Grandma smiled triumphantly. "No returns. That's how come it was a good price."

"Napoleon didn't have a chance against me," Uncle Vittorio chuckled.

"Well, I'm very sorry," Mom continued in a firm voice, "but we simply can't go. You should have asked us first. I'm sure you can find another three people to go with you. You can take your friends instead. That trip doesn't fit our schedule."

The Last Big Fight picked up steam in the car on the way home from Grandma's and continued for quite some time after we got home.

"Your mother is trying to take over our lives!" Mom told Dad.

"Dr. Nickels said we shouldn't exclude her."

"I thought you said Dr. Nickels was incompetent," Mom pointed out.

"My mother doesn't know how to be any other way. She's just doing her best to be friendly."

"HA!" my mom said petulantly.

"All right, all right," Dad said, sounding tired, wilting, ravaged and wan. "I'll tell her we can't go."

Actually, I wanted to go to Disney World with my

parents and Grandma, but I kept my thoughts to myself. Things were already touchy enough.

That was Part One of the Last Big Fight. In the next chapter I'll tell you what happened next. Get ready for some *very* trenchant conflict.

## 9

Before I get to Part Two of the Last Big Fight, I have to fill you in on another birthday party I had, back when I was eight.

My mom didn't want Grandma to come until after the party was over, so she told her to come at three o'clock. But at noon, which was when the kids were all supposed to arrive, the doorbell rang, and it was Grandma. She's no fool.

"Hello! Hello! How is my sweet birthday girl! I hope you don't mind that I came a little early!" She piled all sorts of packages on the table: junk food to eat along with Mom's carob-covered peanuts, and gifts and streamers and balloons and pin-the-tail-on-the-donkey and paper plates with pink flowers on them.

My mom's hair seemed to be turning white on the spot. She had to go out for a walk to cool off.

Then all the kids arrived. Grandma said proudly,

"Now I will teach you a wonderful game. It is called Mother, the Witch Stole Monday."

I was the Mother, because it was my birthday, and Grandma was the Witch and my friends were Daughters (and one Son, Yoshi, who *asked* to come to the party) who were named after days of the week. The Mother, me, went away to run errands — I hid in my room — and the children stayed in the living room. I heard the Witch plead, "Let me have a candle so I can see my way home."

The children gave the Witch one of the candles from my cake, and the Witch stole the children (put them in the kitchen) and turned them into a type of junk food (gave them each something to hold, like chocolate chip cookies). When I came home to the living room, my children were all missing.

"You may have your children back if you guess which child is which food," the Witch said, pretending to cackle wickedly. I only got one right — Wednesday. So all the other kids got to take home the food they were turned into, and Wednesday got to sleep over. Which worked out perfectly, because Wednesday was Genevieve.

Okay, this game is extremely lame, but we were only seven and eight years old, so we didn't know any better. We thought it was great.

Mom reminded Dad about that party during the Last Big Fight. By this point I was in my room, but my mom has a very loud voice. I heard her every word. "Remember when Pauline turned eight? Remember how your mother barged in and took over the whole party? Maybe if you'd said something then, it wouldn't have escalated, year by year, until finally she's decided she can plan our family vacations!"

Dad mumbled something I couldn't make out.

"Maybe once you loved me," Mom accused, "but you don't any more."

"You're not the same person you used to be," Dad commented.

I got nervous when he said that. I was already worried enough about my parents turning into ghouls in the middle of the night.

My mom didn't like hearing that either. "Those words are like a knife in my heart!" she cried out in an agitated, troubled and delirious voice.

At that point I dropped some heavy items on the floor of my bedroom, to remind my parents that there was a child in the house. I guess they got the message, because I heard Dad go up to his studio. Mom stayed downstairs and began singing another one of her songs.

You'd think we were in a musical, the way Mom

sometimes bursts into song. But that's what Mom does when she's stressed out. When you have an ex-opera singer for a parent, you have to expect that.

This song was about some crook who was coming before a judge to have all these trials, and his brothers were trying to help him. He didn't seem too optimistic though. The song goes,

*All my trials, Lord, soon be over*
*Too late my brothers, too late, but never mind*
*All my trials, Lord, soon be over* (illustration 12).

Well, I don't know whether the crook's trials were over, but my parents' marriage was definitely over. They told me so the next day.

I don't think I'll finish this book over the summer. Zane was right. Writing a book is way more work than I'd realized. But that's okay. If I'm not finished by the end of the summer, I can go on writing when school starts.

So long for now!

## 10

Today I went to watch Genevieve practise at the skating ring (rink?). She doesn't like it when I come, because she says it'll be boring for me. But it isn't boring at all, because she's amazing. She was doing some sort of leap and spin today, and even though she did the same thing about seven thousand times, I didn't mind watching her. Her coach, Bruno, is really nice. He's bald and cheerful and very encouraging. He's put on quite a bit of weight since his figure-skating days, but Genevieve says he was once a world champion. She says it's a miracle that she found such a good coach right here in Ghent.

I think I'd probably mind if Genevieve was fantastic at something I was trying to do, but I don't even like skating in a straight line. Or, to put it a little more bluntly, I'm about as good on skates as my dad would be as a talk-show host. Besides, Genevieve's not a show-off.

I don't know why, but it's impossible to admit someone's good at something if they boast about it. But if they don't boast, then you don't mind admitting they're good. Am I making sense?

Genevieve and I go way back. We met at daycare, when Genevieve used to protect me from Tina, the tall girl who's now on the boys' basketball team. Tina grabbed toys from me and tried to tackle me. I guess she was practising for her future career in sports. Genevieve always stood up for me.

Genevieve's actually a year younger than me, but we're in the same grade because of my experience in London with my grandmother, when she sent me to that daycare for intellectually challenged kids. When I returned from London and had to be enrolled in kindergarten, Genevieve and I immediately resumed our old friendship.

Every year Genevieve almost fails. She even does badly in French, which you'd think would be easy for her because of her father. But that doesn't seem to make a difference. The problem is that she has no time to do homework because she's at the skating ring/rink around five hours a day.

At first it was really embarrassing for her to be so far behind at school. I tried to cover for her and to whisper answers to her but the teachers caught on and moved us apart.

Now she's still getting low grades in school, but no one minds that much, because she won First Prize (gold medal) in the Sectionals.

I have one major complaint about Genevieve. I mean, no one's perfect! My major — in fact my *only* complaint — is that she's secretive about the figure skating part of her life. She doesn't like to talk about figure skating, or her prizes, or her gorgeous costumes. And she doesn't want me to come see her perform. She doesn't tell me when the competitions are going to take place, and I've already missed a few really important ones.

When I ask her about it, she always tries to change the subject. The only thing she tells me is that her parents keep complaining that they're going bankrupt from the skating expenses. They say Genevieve is costing them more than all the boys put together, but you can tell they're very proud of her.

But why is Genevieve so secretive about the most important thing in her life? I just can't figure it out. I'm her best friend. We tell each other *everything*. We even tell each other about certain dreams we have (don't think I'm going to tell *you*, I'd rather die!).

And we made a Friendship Pact that when we marry we're both going to get pregnant at the same time so our kids (hopefully both girls) can be best friends too.

But both times when Genevieve won those big competitions she just vanished for a few days, and I had to find out from the kids at school where she was.

I was really mad at her, especially the second time, when she won First Prize and her picture was in the paper.

I made her *swear* that she'd tell me when her next big competition was. I asked her why she didn't tell me, but she just said, "They're really far away, and they last for three or four days. You'd get bored."

"I don't care," I exhorted. "I'll come on the last day. My dad can drive me."

"Okay," she demurred.

"When's your next competition?" I inquired, just to be sure.

"February. That's the Junior Nationals. But you'll be bored," she repeated.

I asked Mom about Genevieve's behaviour. "Maybe Genevieve's nervous about you seeing her in case she doesn't do well," Mom suggested. "You know, when I was in music school, I wouldn't let my parents come to hear me sing at the end-of-the-year recital, in case I goofed. I didn't want them to see it happen."

But that's not the reason. I asked Genevieve, "Does it make you nervous to have people you're close to come and see you perform?"

"Oh, no. I like it. I'm always glad when any of my brothers show up and root for me. That way I know I have people on my side in the audience."

"So why didn't you let *me* come?"

"I told you! It's really far, and you'd be bored."

I don't believe her, but I don't know what the real reason is. I hate not knowing! It frustrates me.

On the other hand, Genevieve is great in other ways. Here's what I most like about her:

1. Never picks a fight
2. Tells me I'm terrific even when I do a bellyflop off the low diving board while she's doing somersaults off the high
3. Great at putting sparkles on black nails, great at hair, likes scary movies, warns me when the gory parts are coming so I don't have to look
4. Never makes fun of me
5. Almost always in a good mood
6. Likes my T-shirt collection
7. Likes to spy on Mrs. Clean with me

I have to tell you about Mrs. Clean, but I'll save it for the next chapter. *Don't confuse the reader with too many topics in one chapter!* Zane warns.

## 11

Mrs. Clean is a very strange person who lives next door to my dad. That's not her real name, but we call her that because all she does is clean.

First I have to remind you about my dad's house. When my parents bought it, it had three bedrooms upstairs, but my parents tore down all the bedroom walls and turned the upstairs into one big room, which is my dad's studio. Then, downstairs, they turned the den into their bedroom, and the dining room into my bedroom. So I'm on the ground floor and I have a nice, big window, as you can see in the drawing I made for you in Chapter Three.

Well, the window in my room looks right into Mrs. Clean's kitchen. The curtains on Mrs. Clean's kitchen window are basically transparent.

I know it's wrong to spy, but we're not hurting anyone. And Mrs. Clean is a very interesting person to watch.

First of all, she's always cleaning, scouring, purifying, disinfecting and ritually immersing. She scrubs the tables, the chairs, the sink, the counter, the cupboards (illustration 13).

And then there's her shell collection. She has a big tin box full of shells and every day she washes the shells and then varnishes them with clear nail polish. Those shells must have a thousand coats of varnish on them.

Her diet is interesting too. She eats jam right out of the jar with a spoon, and grapes, and pretzels. She hardly eats anything else.

My parents would kill me if they knew I was spying. But Genevieve understands the thrill. I mean, here's a chance to watch someone who is really different.

I haven't told you the really weird part yet. Sometimes Mrs. Clean shakes her fists at someone. Only there's no one there. Maybe it's something she hears on the radio that makes her angry. But I've never seen a radio.

I guess I'd feel sorry for Mrs. Clean if she was a nice person. But she isn't. She's irritable, surly and mean.

Every time she sees Stormy Weather (my cat) in her yard, she runs out of her house with a stick and screams, "I will poison that cat! I will poison that cat! Keep that dirty cat away from my yard!"

It's hard to explain to cats about fences, though. Stormy Weather doesn't know she's in Mrs. Clean's yard.

"What if she really does poison Stormy Weather?" I asked Dad in a worried voice.

"Luckily, she's a picky eater," he reminded me. It's true, Stormy Weather won't even eat a different flavour of her usual food if they run out at the store, so she's safe.

My mom tried giving Mrs. Clean a chocolate cake. That was when Mom and Dad were still married. Mom came back still holding the cake.

"She shut the door in my face," Mom fumed.

"She's not really well, Barbara," Dad reminded her.

"I know," Mom admitted. "But does she have to be so rude?"

I'm meeting Leila and Augusta at the mall, so I have to end the chapter now. It's a bit on the short side, but at least I revealed the *hidden truth* about my spying.

ttyl!

## 12

When I first read the advice in *You Too Can Write a Great Novel!* about *hidden truths*, I figured that part would be easy because I'm more like my mom than my dad. Now I realize that I'm not exactly like her. For example, she'd never be embarrassed about her father's name, if he had a strange name, or about what sort of paintings he worked on in his studio.

In fact, it's hard to think of anything that would embarrass my mom.

Maybe she's more confident than I am. Or maybe that's just her personality. She always says, "It's better to let people know the worst than worry about them finding out."

Well, I'm going to take her advice. Besides, I want this to be a Great Novel and Zane says if I want to write a Great Novel I have to *be honest*. I guess if I'm going to be a writer, I have to make some sacrifices, just like Genevieve getting up at 5 a.m. so she can be a figure skater.

So here's the truth about my dad's name and about what he paints.

My dad's name is Pippino.

It isn't my fault.

You'd think if someone had that name they'd change it, but no, Dad is proud of his name. He says it's a very common and ordinary Italian name.

All I can say is, thank goodness the high school kids he teaches haven't found out yet. Dad doesn't teach at Newton, fortunately. He teaches at two schools: a private school called Sir John Crimps Academy for Boys, and a school in London (London, Ontario, of course — he doesn't fly to England every day lol) called Merton High. The Merton kids are apparently a handful.

Luckily, my mom always used to call Dad "Honey" when they were married, so kids who came over didn't find out his real name. And Grandma calls him *mi amore*, so I'm safe when she comes to visit too. What worries me is that one of these days some kid will come over and look at our mail, and see a letter addressed to Pippino Carelli.

Now for what my dad paints.

Shoes.

Old shoes. And slippers. Old slippers.

Almost always on a road or a street. One old shoe or slipper or sandal on a road. My dad has a thing about one shoe on a road.

Not surprisingly, people aren't exactly lining up to buy my poor dad's paintings of old shoes, so it's a good thing he also teaches. Even though, don't get me wrong, he's very good at shoes and roads! He's got excellent technique.

I can't really hide that part from anyone who visits me. Whenever I have friends over, the first thing they want to do is go up to the studio and fool around with my dad's paints and pastels. Dad always has easels set up for me and my friends, and he lets us paint whenever we want to, as long as we clean up.

So Genevieve and Leila and Rachel and Augusta have all seen my dad's old, worn-out, shabby, sordid, pokey and dissipated shoes, both on canvas and in real life. The studio is full of old shoes and slippers, which my dad finds at rummage sales. Augusta was the only one who raised her eyebrows, but that's the sort of thing you have to expect with her. She can act quite superior, but when you travel all over the world and your mother rides horses and you know German from your grandmother and Will Smith has kissed you on the cheek, you have a right to act superior because, let's face it, you *are* superior.

On the other hand, Augusta can be quite pushy. Last winter the Viper gave us this project to do on Suffragettes. Suffragettes were women who suffered by tying themselves to fences with chains so that women would be allowed to vote.

Well, Augusta asked to be with Genevieve and Leila and Rachel and me, but then she told us she was going to join another group. We worked like for weeks on this project, and then at the last minute Augusta informs us that the other group wasn't getting anywhere, so could she come back to us.

We weren't very enthusiastic about taking Augusta back at the last minute, after we'd done all the work without her. But she promised that if we agreed, she'd take us all to California with her, and introduce us to Reese Witherspoon, who's a friend of her cousin's sister-in-law. She assured us that her mother had agreed. The thing is, Augusta really is incredibly wealthy, and she really does go to California about twice a year to visit her relatives, and we know for a fact that she met Meg Ryan at a party, because she showed us a photo of a lot of people at a party and Meg Ryan is there in the corner, a bit blurry but you can tell it's her.

We knew it was a long shot, but we said okay. It's hard to say no to Augusta. She's very persistent, and she can be extremely charming when she feels like it.

But when it was time to bring the project up in front of the class, Augusta ran ahead of everyone, carrying the posters and chains and fake newspaper articles and everything else, and she started acting as if she was the one who had all the ideas. The whole time she kept saying, "*I* thought you'd be interested in seeing what the chains must have looked like" and "Let *me* show you these mock newspaper articles," as if she'd done everything alone!! We were so mad, I can't tell you. And then Ms. Nipuitz gives me and Leila and Genevieve this really dirty look and says, "And what did you girls contribute?" Can you imagine!

And needless to say, the closest we got to California was looking at a postcard that Augusta was kind enough to send us, of three hot guys walking along a beach with their surfboards.

Still, I have to admit that when she got back, she brought each of us a NO RULES ALLOWED T-shirt and extremely cool jelly sandals, blue with glitter inside. So we more or less forgave her. Plus, in the end, she didn't meet Reese Witherspoon either. Reese Witherspoon wasn't even in California. She was off shooting a movie somewhere.

13

The truth I'm going to reveal in this chapter has to do with my mom's house. It's not actually a *hidden* truth. It's more of a *disturbing* truth.

You may have noticed that I've described my dad's place but not my mom's. You might even get the impression that I'm at my dad's most of the time.

Actually, I spend just as much time at my mom's place. But the only friend who's been there with me is Genevieve. When I have other friends over to visit, it's always at my dad's.

"Now, even though we've decided to divorce," Mom told me after the Last Big Fight, "we're going to live within walking distance from each other, and you'll be able to see either one of us whenever you like."

"Why doesn't Dad just move into the studio, and you could stay in the room downstairs?" I suggested hopefully.

"I don't think that'll work," Mom sighed. She looked sad, melancholy, crestfallen and prostrate.

At first, my dad was going to move out and find a new place. But Mom told him, "I want a new place and a fresh start. I don't want to be haunted by memories. I plan to move on. And you need your studio."

So Dad agreed. He agrees to whatever Mom wants, nowadays.

"We're going to buy the house down the street," Mom informed me. "We're very lucky there's something so cheap for sale right next to Dad's."

"I don't remember seeing anything for sale," I intoned.

"Right over on Elm Street," she elucidated.

"Can we go see it?"

"We can look from the outside."

So we put on our coats and boots and walked towards Elm Street.

When my mom pointed to the house, I was quite simply aghast.

"I'm not living there!" I shrieked.

The house was fairly big. That wasn't the problem. The problem was that it was *falling down on one side*! I mean, half of it was sort of leaning over sideways.

Apart from that, it looked decayed, wormy, weevily,

moth-eaten, mildewed and gangrened.

"All it needs is some cleaning up and painting," Mom imparted.

"But Mom, it's FALLING TO ONE SIDE!" I almost shouted.

"Well, Dad took a look this morning and said it won't collapse, and that's the main thing. It was just built a little unsymmetrically. He said the foundation is fine."

"This is the Nightmare on Elm Street," I mumbled.

"Listen," Mom said irritably. "I looked high and low for a place close by. The condos next to the arboretum are all full and there's a huge waiting list. You don't know how lucky we are that this inexpensive house happens to be on sale just now. It's a godsend."

I have to admit I started worrying about Mom when she called this sorry excuse for a house a godsend. Maybe working with former criminals was finally having an effect on her. Maybe she'd lost all perspective and thought it was okay to live in a place that strongly resembled a crack house.

Next thing I knew I'd have to go pick her up from the police station for making a public disturbance or shooting up in a washroom.

And what would my friends think? They'd feel sorry

for me that my mom had gone over the edge. It was obvious I couldn't ever bring anyone over.

But there wasn't any point saying all this to Mom. She wouldn't have taken it well.

The next day, we went to the Rainbow Senior Residence to meet the owner of the house.

His name was Mr. Applewood and he was in a wheelchair that had a tray, and on the tray he had a book, and the book was called *Test Your IQ*. If I'm beginning to sound like Dr. Seuss, it's due to stress.

We met in a big lounge with orange and blue plastic sofas and a TV that was on without any sound. "Hello, there," Mr. Applewood said. He had a loud, booming voice. "I'm a member of MENSA."

"How nice," Mom said politely. She didn't really mean it, but you couldn't tell unless you knew her the way I do.

"What's MENSA?" I asked.

"MENSA, my dear, MENSA!" Mr. Applewood shouted. "Club for people with high IQs! My IQ's climbing every day." He waved the book at me, then let me look at it. It was full of puzzles and brain teasers and those quizzes with four shapes in a row and you have to guess the fifth.

"How nice," Mom repeated. She can be so fake sometimes!

"So you want to buy the old homestead, eh?" he continued enthusiastically. "I built that house with my own two hands, you know, and not a penny in my pocket. I did all the electricity too, but I had to have it redone three years ago when an inspector came. She said she'd never seen such a hazardous wire-up in her life." He began laughing loudly, as if being electrocuted in his sleep was the most hilarious thing he could imagine happening.

When he finally stopped laughing he shook his head. "Anyway, it's safe now. And if you find my scrapbook, please let me know. It's the only thing I lost in the move."

"I'll keep an eye out for it," Mom promised.

"Yup, it's a grand house," he chuckled. "I lived there forty-six years, and all my dogs are buried in that yard. I didn't have a bathroom at first, just an outhouse. I only got that bathroom ten years ago, when I was 74. But I had some help building it, I admit. Didn't have the strength I used to when I was young and hale. That's why I needed a bathroom in the first place. I just couldn't make the long walk to the outhouse in time. Soaked my pants every time!"

I wonder why he thought we wanted to know that. And who says "hale" anyway?

He went back to chuckling. He chuckled so hard he began to choke and my mom had to pat him on the back.

After all the papers were signed, Mom spent a week cleaning up the place. It was so dirty she hired a 17-year-old called Faz to help her. Faz has a partly shaven head and a snake tattooed on his scalp. He's the boyfriend of one of the women in the halfway house Mom works at.

You wouldn't think a punk teenager would be good at cleaning up, but this guy really was. He was about the neatest person I ever met. He even washed the rags at the end of the day and hung them up neatly on the fence.

"My God, I've never seen so much dirt in my life!" my mom ranted at suppertime. We were eating pizza because Mom was too exhausted to cook. Faz ate his slice with a knife and fork, and with a napkin spread on his lap. Maybe I've been wrong about punks all my life!

"I don't think that man ever cleaned at all." Mom shook her head. "By the way, I found his scrapbook."

"Where was it?" I asked.

"Right on the floor, but you couldn't see it under all the dust."

"What's in it?"

"'Letters to the Editor.' From Mr. Applewood to the local paper. Whenever he had a letter published, he cut it out and glued it in this scrapbook."

"What are the letters about?"

"Mostly they're advice to the prime minister on how to run the country. Starting with Mackenzie King, right through to Mulroney, then he must have lost the scrapbook. The only person he skipped was Trudeau. I guess he had no complaints about Pierre Trudeau."

Then she began to laugh, titter and chortle, which would have been fine except that a minute later she was crying, sobbing and lamenting, so that Faz had to get her a box of tissues for her dripping nose.

She wasn't too happy about the divorce.

## 14

Now you know how my mom felt about the divorce.

Here's how my dad felt: composed, unbothered, sedate, eupeptic and bovine. And he says he's never getting married again.

The subject came up last summer, at one of these rummage sales he goes to in search of old shoes and slippers for his paintings. I noticed that a woman wearing a cool Avril Lavigne sort of outfit was definitely looking his way, if you know what I mean. She was pretending to be interested in old shoes too. Usually people her age don't look good if they wear cool clothes, but on her they looked cute.

"Think you'll ever get married again, Dad?" I asked him.

"Nope," Dad replied immediately.

"Why not?" I demanded.

"Once was enough," he commented, picking up a

pair of black rainboots and examining them.

"What if you meet the most perfect person who ever lived?" I asked, glancing at the woman in the Avril Lavigne outfit. For some reason, I liked her.

"Nope." He put the boots back on the table. I guess they weren't worn enough.

"But why?"

"It's just asking for trouble," he said, examining a pair of red sneakers with the soles coming off.

I looked at the woman. She was walking away.

"You know what your problem is?" I told him. "You're antisocial."

"You think so?" he mumbled absently. He always says that when he doesn't know what else to say.

"Well, you're okay with kids I invite over. But you never go to parties or anything. You don't even have any friends. How come you never talk on the phone?"

"I don't like parties. And what about Harry?"

"All you ever do with Harry is play chess! You never even say anything, except 'mate' and 'checkmate.'"

"These are perfect!" he said, digging out an ancient pair of huge brown-and-white men's shoes. Half brown, half white. I've never even seen a pair of shoes like that before. They were truly the winners of the worldwide ugliest shoe contest.

"Grandma says that when you were dragged to a party as a kid you used to hide in the closet and draw."

"She's exaggerating. That only happened once or twice. How much for these shoes, please?" he asked the woman in charge of our table.

"Oh, a dime for those."

"There goes my supper," Dad joked.

Now here's how I felt about the divorce: disgusted, oppressed, offended, inconvenienced and derailed.

My first night at Mr. Applewood's house, which was now my mom's house, was the worst in my life. The whole place smelled of bleach, which my mom had used to clean up the bathroom.

My mom put up a photo of Dad on the wall next to my bed, as if I was two years old! How clued out can a parent get?? I took the photo right off and almost ripped it in half, but I didn't, because it wasn't Dad's fault that Mom was having brain impairment. I just stuck it in Mom's room.

I couldn't fall asleep for the longest time. For one thing, I was used to having Stormy Weather sleep on my feet. I love when she starts cleaning herself, it has a kind of hypnotic rhythm to it and helps me drift off. But she stayed with Dad because Dad likes cats more than Mom, who always used to grumble about changing the litter.

When I finally fell asleep, OMG I had such a horrible dream.

It's a funny thing about dreams. You can dream about vampires and monsters and it can be a sort of interesting and good dream, and you can dream about something ordinary and it can be a nightmare. It's the way you feel in a dream that makes it awful.

Well, that night I dreamt my dad's house was flying in the air and trying to land in a playground, but it couldn't fit in between the swings and the merry-go-round. So then it tried to land on Mr. Applewood's house and become the upstairs. But it couldn't land there either, because Mr. Applewood's house was too run down and would get crushed. Then a swarm of mosquitoes, like millions and millions, began streaming out of Mr. Applewood's house and the house was turning into a swamp and my bed was sinking right into the swamp, which was even more full of mosquitoes. I was trying to hold onto Dad's house to get out of the swamp, but I couldn't. And then it got even more spooky, with all sorts of people in masks … and I was trying to wake up but I couldn't.

I was still scared when finally I woke up. I had to

turn on the light and I never really went back to sleep.

"Do you ever have nightmares?" I asked Genevieve the next day.

"Uh-huh. I have one dream, it's so terrible! I come out on the ice and I've forgotten my whole routine and I just stand there and the music starts. Or else I start my routine and it's the wrong music and I think it's my fault because I've forgotten the routine that goes with the music. And then I look at the judges, and they're my school teachers from Newton. I hate that dream."

Genevieve is the only person I ever invited to see Mom's house. After all, she *is* my best friend, and besides, as I mentioned, she's very non-judgemental and positive.

"Cute," she commented.

That's the word my mom used to describe Faz's shaven head and snake tattoo, so it wasn't much consolation.

"Cute!" I wailed. "I feel like I'm in a movie about orphans in London in 1862!"

"I like that it's old and looks like a farmhouse," she said. "And now you have two houses, which is awesome. You have somewhere to escape to. Just like I come over to your place when my brothers are driving me crazy. Raymond says hi, by the way."

In case you forgot, Raymond is the brother who told us that World War Three had broken out. As he never misses a chance to remind us. He thinks the image of us huddling in the tool shed, terrified that the world was coming to an end, is hilarious. He has his own sense of humour.

"I just can't see this place as a refuge from anything," I sighed.

"At least your parents are still talking to each other," Genevieve said optimistically. "Think of Marianne."

Marianne is a girl in our class who was kidnapped seven times by her parents. First her father kidnapped her, then her mother, then her father again, and so on, back and forth. The only reason they didn't get arrested is because Marianne pretended that she was the one who ran away each time, and maybe also because if they both go to jail Marianne won't have *anywhere* to go. She's always telling us stories about how much her parents hate each other and the things they do to one another. Her mother broke into her father's house and erased all his computer files. Her father sent e-mails to everyone her mother knew including her boss, pretending he was her, and making her sound insane.

So I guess Genevieve's right: I'm luckier than Marianne. But not as lucky as Genevieve.

"Why can't I have parents like yours?" I groaned.

"My parents are so busy bringing up six kids they

never have time to fight," Genevieve replied. "Besides, they aren't allowed to divorce. Catholics are stuck with each other forever."

"Well, I wish my parents were Catholic," I grumbled. Dad had a Catholic upbringing, but he says that if you stop doing churchy things, you stop being a Catholic. Whereas Jews stay Jewish forever, even if they were adopted at birth and don't even know they're Jewish.

"And I wish my dad was an artist with a big studio and my mom watched movies with me all the time."

I forgot to say something else I like about Genevieve: she knows how to cheer people up. I really felt better after I talked to her. I don't know why.

Btw, I found a new T-shirt today. Dark blue with a peaceful looking pink palm tree, and under the tree it says TAKE IT EASY.

Good advice, if your life isn't a sea of troubles.

Well, bye for now!

15

Today a very strange thing happened. I was playing Frisbee with Genevieve and the Frisbee flew into Mrs. Clean's backyard. Usually when that happens Genevieve just climbs over the fence and gets it and very quickly climbs back. It's sort of exciting, actually. Like getting past the witch in a kids' story.

But today the Frisbee didn't just land in Mrs. Clean's backyard — it landed right inside these very thick cedar bushes she has along her back fence, to block out the other neighbours.

So Genevieve climbed over and very carefully tried to push those bushes apart, but she couldn't reach the Frisbee.

Well, out comes Mrs. Clean, carrying a mop. Genevieve made a dash for it and rushed back to our yard. That mop didn't look too promising.

But it turned out the mop wasn't a weapon at all.

Mrs. Clean went straight to the bushes and dragged out that Frisbee with her mop. She didn't touch the Frisbee, though. She just poked it along the ground with the mop until it was in the middle of the yard, so we could get it.

Only we didn't move. We were just standing on our side of the fence, watching her in a bewildered way.

And that was only the beginning. The next thing Mrs. Clean did was even more surprising. She came over to us, and said, "I had two foster-children once. And the oldest just sent me a plant. She lives in Nova Scotia now. Her name's Marlene. I don't know where the boy is. Jail, probably. Always was a good-for-nothing."

Then she turned around and went back to her house.

Genevieve and I were completely speechless.

Sometimes life takes you by surprise and throws you a curve ball. Or, in our case, a curve Frisbee.

Now I feel sorry for Mrs. Clean. I don't think she made up that story, because we really did see a new plant on her kitchen table this week. And who would make up a story about a foster son in jail?

I can barely type, btw, because yesterday I had a pre-test practice in swimming. Maroon is brutal.

They expect you to do twenty laps in a row! But Mom won't let me quit. She'll only let me quit the classes I like.

So this chapter will have to be short. I must lie down and rest my weary bones and aching muscles.

## 16

First day of middle school. It would be my second year in middle school, if my parents had been more responsible when I was five. But, on the other hand, if I had started grade one on schedule, I wouldn't have been in the same year as Genevieve, so I guess I can live with being in the wrong grade.

I didn't work much on this book in August. I wasn't inspired. In *You Too Can Write a Great Novel!* Zane Burbank talks about inspiration. He says: *Don't wait for inspiration, just keep on working.*

That's easier said than done, Zane!

Today I'm inspired, though, because I want to tell you that for the first time since kindergarten I actually have a normal teacher. Here's what Genevieve and I have been burdened with so far:

First grade: Miss Pennington-Rhys. Wore a hat *indoors*, spent the whole year talking about table manners and other kinds of manners. Made us practise eating with forks and knives and saying: "How do you do, Mr. Smith?" Talked a lot about how kids in England were much, much better behaved. Always on my case for daydreaming.

Second grade: Mrs. Pringle. A hundred years old. Treated us like infants. Always on my case for daydreaming.

Third grade: Mr. Bourgeois. Boring, dull, monotonous, tedious, sleep-inducing, sleep-compelling, sleep-inviting, sleep-provoking and sleep-causing. Didn't notice that I was daydreaming.

Fourth grade: Amelia. I don't remember her too well.

Fifth grade: Miss Mary. An ex-nun. Overly sensitive. Cried when Martin Mole threw a paper airplane at her. Never failed anyone. Worst comment on exam (even if you got zero): *Very good effort.* Too nice.

Sixth grade: The Viper. Tried to raise standards of education in the country by overloading, saturating and bloating us with homework and exams and tests and quizzes and reviews and oral presentations and projects and essays and scrapbooks and poems that are ONE HUNDRED AND EIGHT LINES LONG to *memorize.* I'm not kidding! We had to memorize Edgar Allan Poe's "The Raven" — the *entire* poem.

Poor Genevieve, she never got past the first two lines. Most frequent comment on stuff we handed in: *Very poor effort.* Tormented me for daydreaming.

This year we're finally in luck. Our home-room teacher is called Mr. Pete and he's going to be teaching us English, Social Studies, Science and Math.

Mr. Pete is good-natured and accommodating. He has brown eyes that are sort of round and he's thin and a bit short and a bit balding on top, and he has a black beard (one of those very trimmed neat beards). Everyone was quiet and well-behaved, even Martin Mole, because we enjoyed listening to what Mr. Pete had to say.

"We have a lot to cover this year," he sighed. "It isn't going to be easy to get through it all. But we'll do our best, and what will be, will be."

He was really talking to us as though we were his equals and we were all in the same boat. I never had a teacher like that before.

"If you fall behind," he continued, "don't panic. Just let me know, and we'll see what we can do."

Martin Mole raised his hand. "Do we have to ask to be excused if we need to go pee-pee?" He was just trying to be funny. But almost no one laughed. Only a few kids tittered a bit.

Mr. Pete answered very seriously. "Let's take a vote. Whoever thinks you should ask to be excused when you need to answer the call of nature, raise your hands now." About seven or eight kids raised their hands.

"Whoever thinks you should just get up quietly and then return quietly a few minutes later, raise your hand." The rest of us raised our hands.

By then we forgot all about Martin Mole saying "pee-pee." And Martin didn't try anything else. I think he was finally defeated.

"I'm in love," Genevieve moaned when we were dismissed at noon.

"Yeah," I replied. "He's really nice."

"No, I mean *in love*!" Genevieve repeated with more emphasis.

"Now you know how I feel," Leila said dreamily, holding her folder, which is covered with photos of Kalan, to her chest.

"I wish I knew how you felt. I've never been in love with anyone," Rachel sulked.

"He's too old for you, Genevieve," I reminded her.

"I know," she said sadly.

"Maybe he'll wait for you," Rachel said hopefully.

"He's probably married already," Genevieve guessed. "Besides, wait till he finds out what a dummy I am."

"Don't be crazy," I chastised. "You're not a dummy, and Mr. Pete isn't prejudiced."

Then Genevieve went off to practise, her eyes distant and hazy. And now Rachel just rang the doorbell, she asked to come over, so I have to run.

So long for now!

## 17

Why does bad news always follow good news?

The good news is Mr. Pete. The not very good news came last night.

The evening started off quite well, with Rachel's visit. She asked to come over because she says she's starting to feel really bored and claustrophobic in her small apartment with her old grandmother. She told me she wants to watch TV and have a computer like normal kids and she wants to know what's going on in the world. She asked if I could show her stuff on the computer. "Show me anything cool," she instructed me.

So we spent about three hours on the computer, downloading music videos, talking to Leila and Augusta and Yoshi on Instant Messenger, and looking up people on MySpace, though that part was a bit pointless, in my opinion. I mean, if someone's my friend, I already know what their favourite music is, and if they're not my friend, why would I care? I told Rachel MySpace was a magnet for perverts.

This really interested her. "What kind of perverts?" she wanted to know.

"Every kind. But not only perverts. Also foreigners trying to get to Canada."

"Have you ever had a crush on anyone?" Rachel asked suddenly.

"Well, a very long time ago I had a crush on Stanley, the leader of this club I used to belong to. But I've become more cynical since then."

Rachel was very eager for more details, so I told her all about Stanley, the leader of the Jewish Kids Club. Stanley was a very tall guy with shaggy hair and glasses. Unfortunately, he was too old for me. He'd already finished university and he was trying to decide what to do with his life.

Mostly what we did at the club was eat and listen to Stanley. On holidays we ate holiday food (I don't really understand why you have to wait a whole year to eat those foods, they are extremely tasty) and between holidays we had pizza. As we ate, Stanley told us stories.

Stanley could make a story about how he washed the dishes so gripping that you were at the edge of your seat. I don't know how he did it. Whatever he decided to tell us about, he made it sound like the most incredible, amazing thing that ever happened, and you couldn't wait to hear the end. His topics were very broad. He talked about Jews throughout the ages, he talked about his grandmother (he called her Bubbie), he talked about problems he was having with his car, he talked about things that happened to him during the week. He never had a boring day, or even a boring hour. Incredible, amazing things were always happening to him. Or at least, they sounded incredible and amazing when he told us about them. Apart from his storytelling talent, Stanley was extremely cute.

There were about seven kids in the club and we met once a week. However, it all came to a sad end one day when Stanley told us that he had finally figured out what to do with his life, because the thing he was going to do with his life was move to Israel. So that was the end of the Jewish Kids Club. A nice woman called Mrs. Klein tried to take it over, but we couldn't relate to her, and her cookies were too dry.

"Did you ever kiss anyone?" Rachel continued to interrogate me.

"Well, I guess ..." I admitted.

"Who?"

"Yoshi," I was forced to confess. "But that was

ages ago, and it was only once."

"What was it like? And who made the first move? And where were you, I mean how did it happen? I mean … I hope you don't mind my asking," she added, suddenly remembering that in theory it isn't polite to pry.

"I don't mind," I said. Rachel wasn't prying, she was just trying to find out what real life was like. "But there isn't much to tell. We were doing some volunteer work at this food bank and we were both in the storage room sorting cans and suddenly we just kissed, I don't even know how or why we decided. It was nice, but the next time we met we both pretended it never happened. Because … well … I don't know why. It was just a spur of the moment thing."

Rachel stayed for supper, which was spaghetti. That's the only thing Dad knows how to make, but he does a pretty good job. Rachel didn't eat much, though. She said she was on a diet. I hope she's not getting anorexic.

Anyhow, the bad news came after Dad dropped Rachel off. I decided to sleep over at Mom's. She told me she'd bought some marble fudge So Delicious ice cream, so that was an added incentive. Tall people need to eat a lot.

I was just digging into the ice cream when Mom said, right out of the blue, "Honey, I have a boyfriend."

"What!"

"I said, 'I have a boyfriend.'"

"You can't use that word! You're a mother!"

"Okay, what word do you want me to use?"

I thought for a minute. Finally I said, "Casual companion."

"All right, then. I have a casual companion."

"How come now, suddenly?"

"I didn't meet anyone until now. Besides, I wasn't ready."

I didn't say anything. I had extremely mixed feelings about this news. Partly curious, partly sick.

"His name is Griswold," Mom said.

"Griswold!" I shrieked. I grabbed the phone, took it with me to my bedroom, shut the door and called Genevieve.

Her father answered. "Genevieve is already in bed," he said in his French accent.

"It's an emergency," I told him. Genevieve goes to bed early because of her practice schedule, but she doesn't mind being woken if there's something interesting going on.

"Okay, a minute please," her dad said.

"What is it?" Genevieve asked when she came to the phone.

"Guess what! My mom has a *boyfriend!* And his name is Griswold!"

"Griswold?"

"Griswold."

"Poor you!" she exclaimed.

"You mean poor Griswold."

We both burst out laughing. And we continued laughing all day today. We had to try not to look at each other, because every time our eyes met, we would collapse into giggles.

My mom must have a special talent for finding men with horrible names.

I'm going to meet Griswold next weekend. We're all going horseback riding at Martha's farm, which is a place Mom and I have been going to for years. Martha's farm is very different from the place where Augusta's mom keeps her two horses, to say the least. Sort of like the difference between a grade-six talent show and MTV.

Genevieve's going to come too. She's very excited because she loves horses, but the only time she gets to ride is when she comes with me and Mom.

Who knows? Maybe Griswold will turn out to be Mom's Prince Charming, galloping through the forest on his handsome steed. But somehow, I doubt it.

## 18

Yesterday Genevieve and I met Griswold. Things didn't go too well for him.

Mom borrowed Dad's pick-up for the drive to Martha's farm, because her hundred-year-old car is trying to get life-saving resuscitation at the local garage. I wore my T-shirt with the wild horses that my London grandmother, Mom's mother, sent me. It's truly gorgeous, so I only wear it on special occasions.

"Griswold's going to meet us there," Mom said cheerfully.

It was beautiful out. The sky was crystal blue with fluffy white Simpsons clouds, and the leaves on the trees were crimson, vermilion, ruby, gold, apricot, ochre, gilded, flaming and lurid.

"I can't wait," Genevieve said as we drove there.

"Too bad Martha looks like Frankenstein," I commented.

"Pauline!" Mom reproved.

"Okay, so she's better-looking than Frankenstein, but she has a square body and a square head. And she looks as if she could lift a car."

"Farmers have to be strong," Mom said, trying to make me feel bad. It didn't work.

"Where is she from?" Genevieve asked.

"Somewhere like Lithuania," Mom told her. "I'm not sure."

"I wonder why her husband ran off," I mused out loud. Martha's husband left one morning two years ago and never came back.

My mom didn't answer.

Martha's farm is huge. She doesn't have that many animals, just chickens and rabbits, which she eats, plus a couple of goats and a cow. But she has a lot of land, and most of it is forest. There's a trail in the forest, and Martha has five horses. For a small fee, she lets people ride on the trail.

I'm not really good at horseback riding. The minute you get on a horse, you realize two things:

1.  You are much higher up than you thought.
2.  The thing you are sitting on is not steady.

Those two facts make horseback riding a far more challenging experience than people realize.

When we got to Martha's we had to wait for Griswold. He was late, because he got lost.

The first thing I noticed about Griswold was that he has a really small head for his body, as though by mistake the wrong head got fitted onto the wrong body. His head was supposed to go on an elf. Somewhere in the world there's an elf with a very big head.

He also has a weird chin. It looks like it has tiny marbles in it.

And his clothes! The three of us — Mom and me and Genevieve — just wore running shoes and jeans and our bike helmets.

But not Griswold. He was wearing these tall shiny riding boots that went way up, and a real riding hat and even one of those jackets you see people wearing in movies about the past. He looked crazy.

My mom said he was a filmmaker and had won a big prize in Cannes, which is a city in France with a famous film festival. It's pronounced *can*, btw, in case you ever go to a sophisticated party and want to impress someone.

Mom continued talking about Cannes, but I barely listened. I was too busy trying not to look at Genevieve.

Luckily, Martha came out of the house just then. I don't know how long Genevieve and I could have kept ourselves from hysterics.

"So! Hello, hello, welcome," Martha greeted us. She was wearing black pants, black rubber boots and an apron. "The horses are ready and waiting." She looked at Griswold and seemed very impressed by his outfit. "I see you are experienced rider," she said, nodding with approval.

"Yes, I do have quite a history of riding," Griswold said modestly. He had a very childish voice. Mom, what were you thinking? You can't be this desperate!

"Excellent, excellent. Happy just had enema so I give you Baby. If you are sure you are able to handle. He is pony."

"Oh, I'm sure I can handle a pony," Griswold said with confidence. Fake confidence, if you ask me.

"Good, good, because he is not so easy, I cannot give to the girls and my friend Mrs. Bloom."

"Can I have Hunter?" Genevieve asked. She always asks for Hunter, because Martha claims that Hunter is the slowest. Hunter is a white mare with this pathetic scraggly tail that looks as if some animal chewed off parts of it.

Genevieve could easily ride any horse, but she

can't risk having an accident, because of her figure skating. "If Bruno knew I was doing this, he'd kill me," she tells me every time we go riding. I've been sworn to secrecy.

Actually, Hunter doesn't seem to me to be any slower than Attila, who's the oldest and who has some sort of skin disease (Martha says it's not catching). Attila is the horse I always get.

I climbed up on Attila with the help of a step-ladder and Genevieve climbed up on Hunter with a push from Martha, and my mom climbed a skinny mare called Carlotta all by herself. She's surprisingly good with horses.

"Here is Baby," Martha told Griswold, pointing to a tiny pony.

"He looks a bit small," Mom said doubtfully. She sounded upset.

"That's all right, I don't mind." Griswold was trying to be pleasant about it.

I can't tell you how stupid Griswold looked with his big riding boots and hat and jacket on this tiny pony. His feet were only a few inches from the ground. I hoped the poor pony was strong enough to carry him.

I'm not supposed to make my chapters too long,

and I still have to tell you how Griswold fell off his horse and broke his ankle — which was NOT, I repeat, NOT my fault — so I'll start a new chapter.

## 19

"You girls go right ahead," Mom suggested. "We'll follow behind."

I think my mom knew how much Genevieve and I wanted to be alone.

As soon as we were out of sight, we burst out laughing. We were laughing so hard I thought we'd explode. We couldn't help it. We'd been holding it in for at least ten minutes.

We probably would have gone on laughing the whole way, except that suddenly Genevieve cried out, "Look!"

She was pointing to a large toad, sitting happily in the middle of the path, not realizing (of course) that the middle of a path is not the best place to be if you're extremely small and several horses are headed your way.

Genevieve got off her horse (good thing she's an athlete!) to move the toad aside, but it didn't budge, so she bent down and scooped it up in her hands. "Hi, Toady." She stroked the toad's bumpy skin. "I wonder why it doesn't try to escape?"

"Maybe it's a trusting toad," I said.

"Or a golden ager," Genevieve said.

"What if it has rabies?" I asked. I can be really clued out sometimes.

"Toads can't get rabies," Genevieve assured me. She pretended that it was a mistake anyone could make. I told you she was nice.

"I was only joking," I lied. "Help me get down, I want to see." I started to dismount and I practically fell on my head, but Genevieve saved me. She's got some muscles!

"Let me hold it." I took the little toad in my hand. The poor toad didn't put up any resistance. I think it was basically frozen with terror. I imagined it going home to its toad family and telling them about this life-threatening encounter with two giants.

Just then my mom and Griswold caught up with us. Griswold didn't seem so happy any more on that little pony, and no wonder. He looked seriously ludicrous.

"Look what we found, Mom!" I called out.

I carried the toad over to meet Griswold's pony. I thought it might enjoy seeing another very small animal.

I held the toad up to Baby's face.

It's not my fault the toad decided to have a fit of hysterics just at that moment. Without any warning, the toad leapt out of my hand, in what was obviously a desperate effort to escape certain death. Two giants was one thing, but being at the mercy of a Fearsome Beast was just too much for anyone. So the toad jumped and collided with Baby's nose, and Baby reared up, neighed and bolted, leaving Griswold on the ground.

You'd think Griswold's leg was amputated, the way he carried on. "My ankle! My ankle!" he whimpered, as if he'd never be able to walk again (illustration 14).

He was sort of pathetic. But I have to admit I almost felt bad for him. It really wasn't my fault, though. He should never have pretended to be an expert rider.

"You girls stay right here," Mom ordered, as if Griswold was a little kid and we had to protect him. Protect him from what? Kidnappers? Who'd want to kidnap Griswold? "I'll go back and phone an ambulance."

Genevieve lifted the poor toad from the ground. By now it was so traumatized that it just lay limply in her hands.

No one said a word while we waited. Griswold whimpered quietly to himself.

Martha returned instead of my mom. She was riding Carlotta. She dismounted and, with one arm, lifted Griswold and slung him like a sack of potatoes over Carlotta's back.

He yelled and shrieked. "Be careful! OW! OW!"

"Be quiet," Martha said in a voice you didn't want to argue with. "You scare the horses."

Griswold shut up.

Back at Martha's, my mom said there were no ambulances available: the hospital had told her to put Griswold in the car and drive him to Emergency. They'd meet the car with a stretcher.

"I carry you to car," Martha offered generously.

"No, no," Griswold said quickly. "I'll just lean on the two of you." So he limped off with my mom and Martha holding him on either side, and they dumped him in the back seat.

Genevieve and I still wanted to ride. We'd paid for two hours, after all.

"I'll come back for you in an hour," Mom said. "If that's okay with you, Martha."

"Sure, sure, I make them my special mustard tea."

Genevieve and I looked at each other.

"And maybe some rabbit's feet soup."

Our eyes went all wide and round.

"Ha ha! I am making a joke! I have apple cake for girls." She smiled, and I noticed that she has a gold tooth.

My mom drove off, and Martha told us to come to the barn with her to see how Happy was doing after his enema.

Happy looked okay to me. But Martha patted him and said, "Come to Mama! Come to Mama!" Then, I swear, she began to sing him a lullaby in Lithuanian!

Anyway, Genevieve and I finished our trail ride, then we had delicious apple cake with Martha in her kitchen. My mom didn't get back for a long time. She was busy helping Griswold register and get X-rayed and have a cast put on his foot.

## 20

I've been so busy with school, I haven't had time to work on this book. It's hard being a writer and having to do homework at the same time.

Mr. Pete is the first teacher not to complain about my daydreaming.

Not that he hasn't noticed. But he turned it into a compliment. I was staring out the window and Mr. Pete said to the whole class, "It's always the philosopher who looks out the window." And a philosopher is: a sage, guru, giant of learning, colossus of knowledge, mine of information and metaphysician.

Finally, someone who understands me!

I'd be in love with him too after that, except he's not my type.

Anyway, three days ago, he reminded us about the Variety Show. "My students"— that's what he calls us! — "My students, the Variety Show is getting closer."

The Variety Show is a fundraiser that our school puts on every year just before the Christmas break. Parents are forced to pay twenty dollars to sit in folding chairs for three hours and watch a bunch of amateurs trip over each other and make fools of themselves.

"And Mr. Helfut is no longer available to do the video, as he and his family have all moved to Iceland."

Probably to avoid the Variety Show, I thought to myself.

"So," Mr. Pete went on, "if you know of anyone with a camcorder and some professional background, please let me know."

Genevieve and I looked at each other. "Griswold!" we both called out.

Mr. Pete looked at us questioningly. Genevieve said euphorically, "We know someone who's a filmmaker. He even won a prize at Cannes."

"A prize at Cannes!" Mr. Pete was very impressed.

"We'll ask him if he can help out," Genevieve promised.

And that's how my mom found out that Griswold isn't a filmmaker.

I don't know the details. All I know is I told my mom about our idea of asking Griswold to do the Variety Show, and she said, "Good idea."

But today when I came home, she only said, "Griswold's not my boyfriend anymore." She looked tense and a bit angry.

"Great — just when I need him."

"You don't need him," she replied, "because he's never made a movie in his life and he's never even been to Cannes. All he did was take a film course once and make a short video about his landlord not doing any repairs in his apartment and asking too much rent. I saw the video. He knows as much about filmmaking as I do!" (Which isn't much.)

"Oh," I said, trying to sound neutral. It would have been unkind to add, *I told you so.*

"Let's go out for dinner," Mom suggested.

Whenever Mom's in a bad mood, it's good for me — unless she's in a bad mood because of something I do. Or don't do, like clean up after I make myself freshly-squeezed orange juice. It's easy to forget about cleaning up when you have something so mouth-watering waiting for you. Besides, making orange juice by hand is more draining than a person might think.

Anyhow, when my mom's in a bad mood about something unrelated to me, we don't just go to Mario's Chinese Food Buffet. We go to La Bohème, which is a very expensive vegetarian French restaurant. It used to be an ordinary French restaurant, but the owner's daughter went missing in a forest where there were lots of bears, and the owner made a vow to God that he'd never serve meat again if the bears didn't eat her, which they didn't, luckily. So now it's an all-vegetarian menu but it's still very swanky and formal, for Ghent.

There are about seven courses, including a Pause de Chef after the soup, which, my mom explained, is supposed to either wipe out the left-over taste of the soup, or give the chef time to prepare the main course. Mom's not sure which. She was going to ask, but I wouldn't let her.

The Pause de Chef was a tall thin glass with cherry-flavoured ice.

The other dishes, apart from the soup, were spinach pie with fresh basil and ricotta cheese; scalloped mushrooms and pearl onions cooked in cream and cheese; flattened new potatoes in brown butter; a tomato walnut salad tossed with mustard and balsamic vinaigrette; chocolate mousse, and Swedish apple cake (I had the mousse and Mom had the apple cake, but we shared). Everything was incredible. Mario's Chinese also has excellent food, but you don't get treated like royalty or a movie star there.

Suddenly my mom said, "Remember when he fell off the pony?"

She smiled a little to herself.

"Is it true Martha threw him on Carlotta?" she asked me. So I told her that part again.

She smiled a little more to herself, then changed the subject. "How's school, Pauline? You haven't complained once yet this year. What's going on?"

"It's because of Mr. Pete. There's nothing to complain about. He's perfect."

"That's good news. What are you guys doing for the Variety Show?"

"A tango."

"Tango?"

"Mr. Pete is teaching us to tango. We have to do it in pairs."

"How lovely! Who's your partner?"

"Yoshi, who else. He asked me, I couldn't say no." Actually I'm secretly glad Yoshi asked me to be his tango partner. He doesn't look like the type to have sticky hands. If any boy is reading this, here's a tip: most humans on this planet do not — I repeat, do *not* — want to hold hands with a person who has just finished eating a leaky jam sandwich followed by dripping cola and a handful of Gummy Bears, unless that person has first passed his hands under a substance known as *water* ($H_2O$).

"How about Genevieve?" Mom asked. "Who's her partner?"

"Genevieve's pairing with Rachel, because there weren't enough boys to go around. It works out, though, because Rachel's not allowed to dance with boys, and Genevieve doesn't want to dance with a boy because she's in love with Mr. Pete."

"Really!' Mom was interested. She loves gossip.

## 21

Genevieve has chicken pox!

She called me up last night to tell me. "I have the worst news," she wailed. "I have chicken pox."

"Didn't you have it already?"

"I thought I did, and my parents thought I did, but I guess they got me mixed up with one of my brothers."

"At least you get to miss school," I tried to be optimistic.

"This is a disaster!" She was on the verge of tears.

"You mean you'll miss the Variety Show?"

"Pauline, I'll miss at least a week, maybe two whole weeks of practice! Now I may not be able to go to the Nationals." She really sounded worried.

Today in school, Augusta and Rachel and Leila and I had a meeting at lunchtime to think of a way to cheer up Genevieve.

"We could bring her flowers," Rachel suggested. As usual, she was wearing one of the lumpy sweaters her grandmother made for her. It was blue with blue trimming.

"Flowers are too expensive," Leila stated. "Especially this time of year. And I don't think Genevieve's into flowers. Why don't we do all her homework for her instead?"

"That's cheating," I objected. Ever notice that when you feel guilty about something, you have to tell everyone it's wrong? I did Genevieve's homework probably around a hundred times, up until The Year of the Viper. At that point I couldn't even manage my own.

"Besides, what's the point?" Augusta agreed. "She'll have to know that stuff anyway."

"The thing she's most worried about is how long she'll have to stay in bed without practising," I said.

"I know!" Leila interjected. "Let's make her a big calendar. She can cross out each day, and we'll draw a skater at the end."

"But we won't know when the end is," Rachel pointed out. "And if we make it too soon, and she's still sick, she'll feel even worse."

We were all quiet. No one could think of anything.

Then Augusta had a stroke of genius. "I know exactly what she'd like best," she said, her eyes narrowing slyly. "Something from Mr. Pete."

"Great!" everyone approved at once. I think at this point the whole school knows how Genevieve feels about Mr. Pete.

"Let's buy a card and ask him to sign it," Leila suggested.

"Perfect!" I assented. "But do we have any money?"

"I'm low on cash, but I have my credit card," Augusta offered.

"They don't take debit *or* credit at the corner store," Leila said gloomily.

"I have my emergency dollar," Rachel spoke up.

"I think I saw two quarters in my pencil case," I added. "And Martin owes me two dollars from last week."

I found Martin, but he didn't have the money. So Louis lent him the money, and now Martin owes Louis instead of me.

We went to the corner store and looked at their card rack. The problem was, they didn't have a big selection. "There are only two get-well cards here," Leila said. "Too bad we don't have time to go to the mall."

One card was covered with pink flowers and gold hearts. Inside there was a long poem in swirly cursive writing. "How about this?" Augusta asked. "Coming from Mr. Pete, it'll really mean something."

"Too personal," Leila said, shaking her head. "He'll be embarrassed."

"Well, this is even worse," Augusta raised her eyebrows in disgust. The second card showed a cat playing a fiddle. Inside it said, BEFORE YOU KNOW IT, YOU'LL FEEL FIT AS A FIDDLE. "This is seriously lame!"

"We could go to the mall after school, buy a decent card and get Mr. Pete to sign it tomorrow," Leila remarked.

But we were all too impatient. So we ended up buying the dumb card with the cat. "She won't mind what the card's like once she sees who's signed it," Rachel said, and we all agreed.

After lunch, we went up to Mr. Pete.

"Genevieve has chicken pox," I told him.

"Oh, no! Too bad!" He pretended to be very shocked.

"So we thought you might want to send her a card." We showed him the card.

He read it, nodded and said, "Of course, of course!"

Then he wrote in huge letters, THE WHOLE CLASS MISSES YOU, GENEVIEVE and he signed it, "Pete."

It would have been better if he'd written I MISS YOU, but on the other hand, he signed plain "Pete," instead of "Mr. Pete."

We'd all had chicken pox already so it was safe for us to visit Genevieve. We went over to her place straight from school.

Her father opened the door.

"We're here to visit Genevieve," I said.

"Ah, *oui, oui*. She is up there, up the stairs."

We marched upstairs single file. Genevieve was surprised when we all walked in. "Hi there!" she exclaimed. "I look awful." She did look pretty awful, covered with spots.

"The spots will all be gone soon," Rachel reassured her.

"Cool posters," Augusta said, looking around her. The walls of Genevieve's room are covered with posters of famous figure skaters, but her trophies are downstairs in the living room, where her seven thousand relatives can see them when they visit.

"We brought you something," Leila said. She handed Genevieve the card.

When Genevieve read the message inside, she was

happy as a lark, in seventh heaven, on cloud nine, and throned on highest bliss. She just held it in her hands and stared at it. Then she sighed, brought it to her lips, and kissed it.

"Please, control yourself," Augusta said. "There are children present."

"He signed *Pete*," Genevieve said in a far-away voice (illustration 15).

We tried to make conversation after that, but it wasn't easy, because Genevieve couldn't take her eyes off the card. After about fifteen minutes her father peeped in through the door and said, "I regret very much, but Genevieve must rest." He meant we had to leave. So we did.

That was our good deed for the day.

I have lots of math to finish, so I have to go. I'm at my dad's, and while I wrote this chapter, Mrs. Clean was standing on a ladder and washing the ceiling of her kitchen. Now she's washing the light fixture.

The phone's ringing! It's for me, so bye for now.

\* \* \*

Three stars means *time has passed*. Zane taught me that trick. I just thought you might want to know that it was Grandma on the phone. She called to invite me over for lunch on Sunday. Dad paints on Sundays, so she said I should come with Mom. My mom and Grandma get along really well now. You'd think Grandma would take Dad's side, after my mom was so unfriendly to her all these years. But Grandma is on Mom's side, maybe because her own husband walked out on her long ago. Mostly they like to talk about my dad's childhood and what he was like then. They both sigh a lot when they talk about him.

## 22

We got through the Variety Show, and in only one week we get off for Christmas break.

Christmas is a pretty pathetic holiday in our family. Since my mom's Jewish, the only part of Christmas she's interested in is the presents and the pretty lights going up everywhere. And Dad is "against organized religion." He's extremely disorganized himself, always throwing his art rags on the floor of his studio and leaving dishes in the sink. I used to think he meant that he'd feel out of place in a church, where everything is neat and spotless. But it turned out that he was talking about the way religions organize your faith for you. Dad prefers to decide about his faith on his own. He's an individualist.

At first, when I was three or four, Dad did his best to get Christmas going for my sake. He bought a tree and some boring decorations at Zed-Mart, but the only member of the family who was excited about having a tree was Stormy Weather. She liked making the bottom branches of the tree move with her paw. She's so cute!

After a few years of this half-hearted tree business, I told Mom and Dad that it was okay, the tree at Grandma's and our family dinner there were enough for me. I think they were both relieved. So now we go over to Grandma's at Christmas and I get to see my Montreal cousins, and I get to eat the most divine food on the planet. My mouth is watering just thinking about it.

Genevieve is over her chicken pox, but she's still recovering her strength, so she missed the Variety Show. Which was fine, because she was supposed to be Rachel's partner, but in the end, when Rachel's grandmother found out that the dance was a tango, she said Rachel wasn't allowed to do it, even with another girl.

I hope you don't think Rachel's grandmother is some sort of ogre, btw. She's actually very friendly and pleasant. Which is more than I can say for my mom! Lately she's been short-tempered, moody and bilious.

Everyone loved our tango! We were the highlight of the Variety Show. Yoshi only stepped on my foot twice. He wasn't totally following the music, but I was right about his hands. They weren't sticky.

The Viper made her class sing "Bird on a Wire." Except that it's supposed to be a song about love (I think) and she turned it into a song about how students will be sorry if they don't study until they go blind. Her students were forced to sing:

*Like a bird on a wire*
*Like a child playing with fire*
*I've ignored every teacher who reached out to me*
*But since it won't be very long*
*Before I see that I have done wrong*
*I will work so much harder for thee.*

I don't know how Leonard Cohen would feel about that change. He's the guy who wrote the song. My dad has the CD, that's how I know the real words (illustration 16).

I phoned Genevieve to tell her about the show, and also about what Mr. Pete wants us to do over the vacation.

"We have to do presentations in January," I divulged. "We're only allowed one partner. We have to pick a topic that's educational, and we have to think of an interesting way of teaching the class about it. We can't just go up and read an essay or anything like that.

We have to be creative."

"Oh, Pauline!" Genevieve burst out. "Ours has to be the best one. We've got to be fantastic!"

She really wants to impress Mr. Pete, of course.

"I was thinking," I continued. "How about opera?"

"Opera?"

"My mom once studied to be a soprano. She has tons of material, and she could even come and sing some famous parts."

"Pauline, you must be joking. Everyone will go into convulsions laughing! Even my parents laugh when they hear opera on the radio."

"I didn't think of that," I sighed.

Genevieve's better than me at knowing the pitfalls of popularity. She's not as good as Augusta, but she's better than me, and she's saved my life a few times. Once, in second grade, I came to school wearing a bracelet I'd made out of beans. She caught me just in time and warned me to put it away or I'd be history. Another time we had a costume party contest and I had this idea of coming as a farm, with little animals attached to my arms and legs. Genevieve rescued me that time too.

"Maybe we could play some Broadway songs?" Genevieve suggested.

"The thing is, it has to be educational. Mr. Pete stressed that a few times. I don't know if Broadway music would count. I could ask him tomorrow," I offered.

"No, no, let's not take a chance," Genevieve replied quickly.

"Well, how about we do opera without singing?" I proposed. "I mean, operas have really dramatic stories. We can act out the story and wear costumes. My mom could help us. She knows all about it, from her opera days."

"That sounds awesome! Especially if I can fall off a chair and die," Genevieve said dreamily.

"Oh, people are always dying in operas," I assured her. "They fall in love, and then they die. That's almost all they do."

When I got off the phone, I told my mom, "I need an opera that has dying in it and is easy for two people to act out."

"I have a book of opera plots," Mom said sleepily. She was stretched out on the sofa with her arm over her eyes. She'd had a hard day. One of the women in the halfway home got arrested for stealing a mug that said BARBARA on it, which made my mom feel awful, because the mug was supposed to be a Christmas present for her. "Look through that book, and choose an opera you like. It's green, it's on the bookcase some-where. Unless it's still at Dad's."

My mom left a lot of stuff at Dad's. Some of it is in the den, in boxes marked BARBARA (like the mug), and some of it is in the unfinished basement. The laundry room is down there too. The entire basement gives me the creeps, actually. It's where my parents' divorce began, with all those fights about the laundry. And it's also where the divorce ended, with Mom dumping her things there.

"It's here!" I called out when I found the book. I looked through the plots, then called Genevieve again. "I think I found one. Tell me if you like it."

"Okay," Genevieve replied.

"We can't go into all the details, but here's the main idea. This evil guy, Lord Henry, wants his sister Lucia to marry some friend of the King so that he can get on the King's good side. The problem is that Lucia is in love with handsome Edgar. Henry wants to kill Edgar, so Lucia goes to warn him, and Edgar says not to worry, because he has to go to France anyway. Then, while Edgar's in France, evil Henry fakes a letter saying that Edgar is in love with another woman. So Lucia agrees to marry the King's friend. When Edgar comes back —"

"He thinks Lucia doesn't love him, right?"

"Right. So he returns this ring she gave him. And she's so upset she goes round the bend, and kills her new husband, and sings off-key. Then she dies and Edgar hears about it —"

"And he kills himself?"

"Right."

"Like Romeo and Juliet …" Genevieve sighed deeply.

"I have an old bridesmaid gown of my mom's for Lucia," I said. "And for Edgar we'd need tights and a lace shirt, that's what guys wore back then. There's a picture in the book."

"Oh, which one should I be?" Genevieve moaned helplessly. "I look good in tights, but maybe I should be Lucia, with a long flowing gown? What do you think Pete will like best?" Ever since we gave her the get-well card, Genevieve refers to Mr. Pete as Pete — not in class, of course, but when she's talking about him.

"Mom's dress would be a bit big on you," I said. "I think you'd look fantastic as Edgar. He also has a much more dramatic death. He throws himself on his sword."

"Oh, that's perfect," Genevieve shrieked joyously. "I'll fall off a chair and die horribly. Maybe I really will faint! Then Pete will have to lift me in his arms …" her voice trailed off.

"My mom told me that in the part where Lucia loses her mind, the guy who wrote the opera used an instrument that makes a high, squeaky sound. Mom said we could make the sound by filling glasses with water. She said some singers refuse to sing with that instrument, because the way it sounds really does drive them crazy. How about we bring glasses to class and make the sound?"

"Good idea. And I think I have a sword from my brother's Master of Slaughter Hallowe'en costume. The only thing is," Genevieve said apologetically, "I won't have all that much time to work on it. I really need the holidays to get back into shape and catch up on the two weeks I missed."

"I don't mind," I assured her. "All I have to do is write a few lines about the history of opera and Donizetti's life."

"Who?"

"He's the person who wrote this opera. It's called *Lucia de Lammermoor*, by the way. Isn't that a fantastic name?"

"Uh-huh. But, listen, you don't mind doing all that work?"

"Writing's my strong point," I reminded her. "I'm getting lots of practice writing my novel."

Which is true, except that I still don't know for sure if I'm doing it exactly right. This chapter, for example. Is it too long? I wish I could ask someone. But I don't really want to show this book to anyone until I'm finished.

Gotta run, *Lost* is on!

## 23

I haven't written recently because I had a body-altering flu. I got it in the middle of Grandma's Christmas dinner. My cousins were there, and two aunts and an uncle and some other people I'm related to but I'm not sure how. It was very crowded. First I was hot, then I had chills, then right in the middle of supper I ran to the bathroom and threw up all the chocolate-covered marzipan I had before dinner. We had to leave early. Grandma was really sad, because we didn't get to try out all the courses, but Dad promised to come back the next day to help finish the leftovers. He can be quite unfeeling.

I was sick for a whole week. I told Mom and Dad I needed a doctor but they said it was only a flu and would pass. They didn't even bother taking my temperature! I had to take it myself. In fact, I had to remind Dad five times to buy a thermometer, because he couldn't find his, and Mom didn't buy a new one when she moved out. Finally Dad bought a thermometer and I took my temperature. It was 38.2 which is 1.2 degrees above normal. I told Dad, but he only said, "As long as it's below 39 there's nothing to worry about." In other words, I have to be at death's door before my parents will get me medical attention. One day it will be too late.

I really felt awful. I couldn't eat, I tossed and turned all night, and I was bored and weak all day. On New Year's Eve Genevieve had a party at her place, but she said it was better if I didn't come, as she couldn't afford to get sick again, she'd already lost too much practise-time. That's why she also didn't visit me. It's a harsh world.

So I ended up spending New Year's Eve in bed with only Stormy Weather to keep me company. Yoshi called just before midnight to wish me Happy New Year, but he couldn't visit because he was in Ottawa visiting relatives. Dad was upstairs painting and I don't know where Mom was. She didn't answer the phone or return my calls, even though I left about twenty messages on her machine.

Finally, two days before my birthday, I found I was feeling a little better. Dad brought home some Indian food and I noticed that I was actually quite hungry. I ate about five platefuls of rice, delicately flavoured with mild *sag aloo*. Dad said he was glad to see me back to myself.

24

Yesterday was January 4. I turned 14, but I couldn't celebrate because we had our first big snowstorm. Probably because of the greenhouse gases destroying our planet, we didn't get any major snow in November and December, only a few snow showers that melted the next day. However, when winter finally decided to come, it had to be in a big crazy storm with ten centimetres of snow by the time it ended. Do not go gentle into that good night!

That's the title of a very catchy poem Mr. Pete taught us, by Thomas Dylan or Dylan Thomas, I forget which. It's a metaphor. A metaphor is when you say something ordinary like "night" but what you really mean is something deeper, like "death". Or when you say "a field of daffodils," and what you really mean is "vegging out on the sofa thinking about good times in the past."

Because of the snow (a metaphor for "having to wait"), I celebrated today instead of yesterday. I didn't want a party or anything like that. I'm too old. So Genevieve and Leila and Rachel and me all just hung out at the mall and then we went to Rock-a-Pie. I would have invited Augusta too, but she's in Cancun, Mexico, at the moment, soaking up the sun at an exotic five-star resort.

Leila talked non-stop about Kalan. As we dug into our scrumptious pies, we were forced to hear in detail about Kalan's eyes, Kalan's mouth, Kalan's smile, Kalan's soul. Leila can tell he has an angelic, tragic soul, and if she had only one wish it wouldn't be for world peace, or to live forever, or to have a zillion dollars, but for Kalan to be in love with her so she could spend the rest of her life with him.

Genevieve lamented, "My situation is way more hopeless than yours." She means Mr. Pete, of course.

"Are you kidding? There isn't a chance in a million I'll ever even be in the same room as Kalan, and he wouldn't even notice me if I was. He can have his choice of any girl in the universe — why would he go for me?" Leila replied vehemently.

"But at least he's your age. You could get trapped on an airplane or something," Genevieve said competitively.

Zane says it's okay to use "said" if you add an adverb. Which is a good thing, because I am running out of synonyms for "said."

"He'd be travelling First Class," Leila said gloomily.

"I wonder how old Pete is?" Genevieve said dreamily.

"At least thirty," I said helpfully.

"He could be twenty-eight," Rachel said consolingly.

"That means that by the time I'm eighteen he'll be at least thirty-four. For sure he'll be married by then," Genevieve said pessimistically.

"I don't think he's the marrying type," Rachel said factually.

We know by now that Mr. Pete isn't married, because he mentioned it. He told us he was hoping to adopt a kid, but it might be hard because he wasn't married.

"What about you, Pauline?" Leila said slyly. "How's Yoshi these days? Any more developments?"

Unfortunately, in a moment of weakness I told her about the storage room kiss. And of course Genevieve knows. Now they all had ammunition against me, including Rachel.

"I have no interest in love," I said blithely. "I'm carefree and independent."

For some reason, that made all three of them burst into laughter. I don't see what's so funny about wanting to spare myself the inevitable cycle of hope and faith followed by betrayal and disappointment.

As for Mr. Pete, I'm really not sure what Genevieve sees in him. He's very sweet, but I don't think he's the type most girls would go for. But Mom says these things are always a mystery. She told me that one time, when she and her best friend Hermione were in university, they were sitting in the cafeteria and this guy walked by. And Hermione said, "Oh God, look at that guy, I want to marry him!"

And Mom thought she was being *sarcastic*, because to Mom he looked sort of skinny and gangly and awkward and he had big ears. She was sure Hermione was joking around, and she said, "Oh, me too, we're really going to have to fight over him."

But Hermione wasn't joking at all. She was totally smitten. So right there and then, she got up and went over to this guy, who got so nervous when he saw her that he dropped his tray. And that's the guy Hermione ended up marrying (illustration 17)!

Mom never told Hermione that she thought Hermione was being sarcastic. "Thank God she didn't find out," Mom said. She and Hermione tell each other everything on the phone, but Mom says the one thing you must never tell someone is that you don't like their boyfriend or husband. The other thing Mom says you can't tell best friends is how they should be bringing up their kids. Too bad, because that's an area in which my mom could definitely use some tips, especially when it comes to endless nagging. I don't see how it's necessary to throw a fit over a measly pair of socks on the floor, for example.

As for Hermione's husband, now Mom keeps saying how smart Hermione was to choose such a generous and straightforward and funny guy, even if he had big ears, while she herself went for a handsome, complicated artist.

After we finished our delicious pies — I had the mixed berry, everyone else had the double-apple — and ice cream, Dad picked us up and drove us home. Dad has a pick-up truck instead of a car because he's always transporting things for his classes. (Zane says *never* to say "things" when you can be specific, but I don't really pay much attention to what Dad takes to his art classes, so I can't be specific this time. Sorry, Zane!)

The pick-up is quite old, but the passenger part seats five, so it's useful for giving me and my friends lifts.

It was slow going, though. The main streets have been cleared, but there's a lot of snow packed up pretty high on both sides.

"Every year it's the same thing," Dad shook his head. "There are always some drivers who don't believe it's going to snow, and don't get snow tires until they nearly kill everyone on the road." He was talking about the car in front of us, which was slipping and sliding because it didn't have snow tires.

I guess in honour of my birthday, he was being chatty for once.

"By the way, Yoshi came over with a present for you," Dad added.

Just what Genevieve and Leila and Rachel needed to hear! They began giggling like infants. Oh, why are parents so tactless?

All in all, it was an okay birthday, even if we didn't do much. Here's my loot:

From Genevieve: a funny T-shirt that shows a cartoon kid named Pauline (she's wearing a T-shirt with her name on it) getting the Nobel Prize for her novel. Genevieve ordered it specially for me on the internet.

From Leila and Rachel: a cute change purse with pink fur.

From my grandmother in London: a T-shirt and a

novel by someone called Faye Weldon. The T-shirt has a picture of a man with a big beard and the words, YOU HAVE NOTHING TO LOSE BUT YOUR CHAINS underneath. Mom sighed when she saw it.

From Yoshi: a CD he burnt of songs he chose for me. I haven't had a chance to listen to it yet.

From Grandma: I don't know yet. She said she'll give me my present when I come over. It's probably a hat and scarf and mitts. She's very upset that I don't wear a hat and scarf and mitts in winter. How can I explain to her that *no one* wears those things?

Mom says it's the fault of the Fashion Industry. "They design fashions for California, and everyone else can just freeze to death for all they care." My mom thinks the Fashion Industry should be like a grandmother, designing warm woollen clothes for everyone. Get real, Mom.

From Mom: the gorgeous white dress I asked for, the blue and pink bracelet I asked for, and a book called *The Struggles of Famous Writers* that I asked for.

From Dad: the same dress, the same bracelet and the same book. I wish they'd discuss these things beforehand.

The only horrible part of my birthday was when my mom said, "That's the year I got my period, when

I was fourteen." Does she think I need to know that? What is it with parents? Don't they have any sense of propriety whatsoever? I will never, ever, ever, ever, ever say anything that tactless to my children, if I have any, which, frankly, I'm beginning to doubt.

## 24

My entire life has been ruined.

How's that for a short chapter, Zane! Ha!

25

I will NEVER, EVER speak to Augusta again! NOTHING she could ever think of or do to bribe me will work. This is the end. The finale of our friendship. If you can even use the word *friend* for a person who is a gossip, a character assassinator and basically an insensitive LOUT.

Well, since everyone now knows, thanks to MS. LOUDMOUTH, I might as well tell you too. I mean, as long as my life is on display for everyone to see, mock and entertain themselves with, you might as well join in on the fun.

Actually, I don't think my readers are as sadistic as the members of my class. I think my readers are going to be understanding, or at least a little bit human, which is more than I can say for 90% of the students at Newton!

Okay, I'd better start at the beginning.

Augusta's parents were planning a post-New Year's party. On New Year's Eve they were soaking up the sun in Cancun, as I already mentioned, but they didn't want to miss out on having a party at home, too. They probably wanted to show off their tans. Augusta invited three friends. The party was for adults, but Augusta and her older sister Sophie, who's sixteen, were allowed to have their own little party in the TV room upstairs.

So Augusta invited me and Yoshi and this guy Clyve that she's crazy about and who goes to Sir John Crimps Academy for Boys, the private school Dad teaches at. I have no idea why Augusta invited me, I'm not really on her list. Maybe she had to invite me because she wanted to invite Genevieve. If Augusta can't wear fairytale outfits and spin in the air with a million people watching and get her picture in the paper, she can at least be friends with someone who does.

Only, Genevieve couldn't come because she's practising like mad and has to go to sleep early, so Augusta was stuck with just me. Even though I'm not on Augusta's main list, I'm probably on a back-up list, along with Leila and Rachel. One thing she likes about us is that we're totally non-threatening. But that's exactly the problem! When you're non-threatening, you can turn into a victim overnight. I should have known better

than to go to that party. Of course, if I *hadn't* gone …
but I won't jump ahead.

Sophie — Augusta's sister in case you forgot —
only invited one guy, Adam, who's in his last year at
Pierre Elliot Trudeau High. His family's from Trinidad.

You should see Augusta's house. It's just like her:
pretentious and ostentatious.

Oh, who am I kidding? It's gorgeous! I wish we had
a winding staircase and marble floors and two fireplaces
and art from all over the world and … never mind,
I'm not going to torment myself.

I showed up at around eight with my mom, who
was also invited. Mom looked presentable for once, in
this black curvy jacket-top and matching skirt and
sparkly high-heels from her opera days. But Augusta's
mother looked like a Vogue model. She was wearing a
long velvety deep-red gown, with tiny beads on the
straps and edges. Her arms were bare. I told you she
wanted everyone to see her tan!

Augusta had told us to dress casually, but I wanted
to wear the white dress I got for my birthday and I'm
glad I did, because it turned out that Augusta's idea of
casual was a pearl-grey three-piece outfit with a silk
vest that her mother got for her in Paris.

The adults were already getting into the mood,

so Augusta and I escaped to the TV room upstairs, with its theatre-sized screen and comfy sofas. Clyve and Adam and Sophie were already there, and a few minutes later Yoshi showed up.

I guess I'm really slow. It took me until I was actually *at* the party to realize that I was being paired up with Yoshi. Can you believe I didn't figure it out until Yoshi walked into the room and I noticed that Augusta and Sophie were busy flirting with Clyve and Adam respectively?

There were lots of snacks in the TV room. Not the usual junk food — these were more high-class snacks, like cashew nuts and shelled pistachio nuts and party sandwiches made with olive bread, and even caviar, which is the only thing I didn't try, because if you know what caviar actually is, it more or less loses its appeal. Augusta completed the spread by bringing in a tray of glasses filled with a very attractive red drink. "These are Cherry Cheesecakes," she said graciously. "They're made with vanilla schnapps and cranberry juice — perfect for the New Year."

I don't usually drink, because the last time I had wine I felt sick after two sips. I think I may have inherited my mom's allergy to alcohol. Also, I'm not really keen on the taste of most drinks. But I decided to give this one a try because it was so pretty, and who can resist anything called Cherry Cheesecake? To my surprise, it was quite tasty, quite tasty indeed.

"Want to play Pile the Kids?" Augusta asked, putting down her empty glass.

"Okay," her sister said in a casual, blasé tone of voice. No one else knew what the game was.

So Augusta and her sister pushed this big bureau away from the wall, leaving a space just wide enough for a kid to lie down in.

"Okay, what we do is, we all pile on top of each other in this space. And we pick numbers out of a hat to see who gets to be at the bottom, who goes next, and so on."

That was only the beginning. After Pile the Kids we played Guess Who Kissed You, Tell Me Your Secret and Pretend I'm Your Puppy.

Good thing Rachel wasn't there!

Then Sophie shut the lights and put on this CD that has only slow sappy songs that you dance to, including some songs from the far past that my parents listen to, like "The Sounds of Silence." Sophie and Adam started dancing, and Augusta and Clyve started dancing, so Yoshi and I sort of had no choice and we started dancing too.

I guess I should tell you that I've known Yoshi since first grade. I don't remember when exactly he started coming over, but it was probably around fourth grade. The thing is, he's really into art, and he was always asking my dad for advice. What size paintbrushes should he be using? What's the best way to get pale blue? How do you stretch a canvas?

Yoshi even asked for private lessons, but my dad said he was too exhausted from teaching his regular classes and he needed the weekends off. Merton kids are not easy to teach. Last week one boy taped his leg to the leg of a chair with masking tape. He said it was an "installation piece." Another time three kids took the door off its hinges and laid it down flat on the floor. They said it was "revolutionary art." I think Dad has some problems with class control.

Anyway, I got used to having Yoshi around. And I got used to the idea that he mostly visits me in order to get free tips from my dad.

The thing about Yoshi is that it's hard to know what's on his mind. He's a very quiet type, sort of like my dad. His mother is a pediatrician, and his father works for some big company. I've never once been to his place, because he never invited me. Why? You can tell there's something he's not telling anyone.

As for the kiss in the storage room of the food bank,
I think it came as a complete surprise to both of us.
We were probably inspired by our altruism and self-
sacrifice. People often have romantic relationships in
heroic times. Besides, speaking strictly for myself, all
those containers of canned peaches and animal crackers
were making me hungry, and since I wasn't allowed to
eat any of it, I had to satisfy my longing some other way.

I didn't really like dancing with Yoshi in Augusta's
den. It was okay when we were doing the tango for the
Variety Show but obviously this was different. It was
actually sort of embarrassing, because it was so set up.
I mean it wasn't spontaneous, it was like we were obey-
ing Augusta's plans. And, to be perfectly honest, Yoshi
is quite a few inches shorter than me.

My mom once told me that when you're embarrassed
and you say it out loud, you feel less embarrassed. I
decided to take her advice.

"This is a bit embarrassing," I said in a low voice.
The music was on pretty loud, so I wasn't worried
about being overheard.

"I know," Yoshi agreed. "How about we go out for
a walk?"

"Brilliant idea!" I said with relief.

I went over to Augusta and asked if I could borrow

a pair of jeans. I told her Yoshi and I were going out for a short walk.

"Oh *good idea*," she said in a knowing voice, which was even more embarrassing, and which should have warned me about what was coming. But it didn't.

So she lent me a pair of Sophie's jeans, since Sophie is more my size, and we put on our winter coats and went out.

It was really magical outside. There wasn't any wind at all and the air was totally peaceful. It was also really beautiful. Under the streetlights the snow sparkled, glittered and twinkled.

"Gorgeous!" I sighed.

"Makes you feel like an antelope," Yoshi answered, which, I admit, is a pretty weird thing to say, but I guess artists have a certain way of looking at things.

Then without any planning at all, we both decided to kiss again.

All right, I guess we shouldn't have had all those Cherry Cheesecakes. Then maybe we would have noticed that we were being watched from behind the bushes by Augusta, Sophie, Clyve and Adam. Maybe after we kissed, Yoshi would not have climbed up to where the tree divides into two and he would not have stood there singing "I Did It My Way" in a very loud voice.

Maybe I would not have started doing expressive dance moves to the words of the song — *which was supposed to be a joke*, btw (illustration 18).

Then maybe the next day when we went on Instant Messenger we wouldn't find out that the *entire school* (since everyone talks to someone) was sharing a whole huge lying version of what happened. Several people would not have changed their chat names to ***I did it my way*** and ***they did it their way*** and ***move over sinatra*** and other such staggeringly brilliant displays of wit. When we got to school there would not have been huge letters on the side blackboard, saying MORE, MUCH MORE THAN THIS. The school desktop would not have been flashing the lyrics of that song, with a picture of two lunatics in a fifties car in the corner.

Well, I'm going to sleep now. I'm exhausted from coping with what are obviously the most immature kids in this country.

Good night.

## 26

Why why why does everything happen to me?????

As if things weren't bad enough already!

First, in school the campaign to destroy my life is getting worse, even though Yoshi and I are completely ignoring each other. Here are only a few of the tortures I've had inflicted on me:

a) A rumour was spread (via chat, e-mail and live action) that Yoshi and I were seen coming out of the boys' bathroom (or in some versions the girls' bathroom) together. This is a flagrant falsehood!! Why would anyone *make up* something like that?

b) A rumour was spread that Yoshi and I spent New Year's Eve in Sophie's boyfriend's car. I didn't even know he *had* a car. And the party was a week after New Year. On New Year's Eve, if you remember, I was lying limply in bed with the flu.

c) A rumour was spread that Yoshi and I were

reading the Kama Sutra. Do you know what that *is*? Leila had to tell us. Kama is this Hindu god of love and Sutra is this like Hindu religious book and the Kama Sutra is a *sex manual*! The kids who invented this particular rumour were so ignorant they think the Kama Sutra is *Japanese* and that Yoshi carries it around with him all the time.

d) The most abominable rumour of all is that Yoshi is teaching me to be a geisha girl, which on top of everything else is in my opinion deeply racist, as is c), now that I think of it.

I'm telling you, there are some very warped people in my school.

And Augusta is actually pretending that she didn't think I'd mind!

Sure, Augusta, I just love to have my privacy invaded. I just love to be exposed to snickering, sneering, sniggering, smirking and lampooning. I just love to have my relationship ruined and destroyed. I just love to have the most personal events of my life exposed, brought to light, laid open to scrutiny and exhumed.

Genevieve and Leila are doing their best to stop the flood, but the waves are just too powerful. As for Rachel, she's hiding in the library, pretending to be immersed in the history of Ancient Greece.

However, she took a keen interest when Leila explained the Kama Sutra to us, and she even asked Leila if she had a copy.

You'd think all this would be bad enough. You'd think I'd gone through just about as much as one human soul can be expected to survive. But no. Today, as I dragged my wan and weary body home to my mom's and collapsed on the sofa in a state of near semi-consciousness, Mom announced that she has a new boyfriend.

I think I was ready to give up at that point and ask my parents to send me to boarding school in Alberta.

Let me fill you in on my mother's latest inappropriate behaviour. I didn't have a chance to tell you that at Augusta's parents' party I noticed my mom talking to a very tanned and slightly handsome man. He was way more tanned than Augusta's parents, who really only looked tanned next to the rest of us sun-deprived Canadians. Compared to the man my mom was talking to, Augusta's parents looked like people who understood the dangers of too much sun.

Anyhow, on that fateful night, after Yoshi and I heard the hysterical laughter coming from behind the bushes, I ran back to Augusta's house, found my mom and begged her to take me home. She was still talking to the tanned man. She wasn't too thrilled about leaving, but she gave in when I told her I was feeling dizzy and a little faint. Which was true at that point.

I didn't see my mom the next day, Sunday, because I wanted to stay at my dad's, in case Yoshi came over to visit, which he did. (Good thing I have at least one presentable home.) Mostly we listened to music while holding hands. Yoshi also showed me how to play Tetris, which I must say is quite addictive. After that we went on Instant Messenger and that's when we found out that we were now its stars.

So today, just when I'm hoping for a bit of a break after an excruciating day, I go over to my mom's, because I haven't seen her in a while, plus I was in the mood for a cinnamon and apple kugel I knew she'd made, and she tells me, "I have a new casual companion."

"Well, good for you," I said rudely. "What's he called — Dracula?"

"No, he's called Bernard," my mom said. You could see she was trying hard not to take my response too personally.

At least it's a normal name for once, I thought, but I didn't say anything out loud. Then it dawned on me. "You mean the guy you were talking to at the party?"

"Yes."

"With the tan, right?"

"I guess so," Mom said pleasantly. "Is this enough lettuce?" She was making a salad for supper.

"If there's only two of us," I said.

"Of course," Mom sounded surprised.

"I thought maybe Bernard was coming to dinner."

"I'd ask you first," Mom said indignantly. "Didn't I ask you about meeting Griswold?"

"No, you asked me whether I wanted to go horse-back riding with you and Griswold. That was a trick question."

"I'm sorry you feel that way," Mom said in a hurt voice that was supposed to make me feel bad. Then she softened. "Bernard's nicer," she promised.

Why do I get the feeling that those two words, "Bernard's nicer," fall into the category of Famous Last Words?

## 27

I told you!! I told you Bernard wouldn't be an improvement on Griswold, and I was right. Bernard spent all of Saturday and Sunday with us. He told us he's a poet, but that for a living he writes descriptions of things in catalogues so people will want to buy them. He showed us one of the catalogues. I have it right here on the table. Here is one of Bernard's descriptions: *Relax and feel yourself swept into utter serenity like a pure Mediterranean breeze as your body settles into the yielding curves of this beckoning chair, perfect for living room and patio alike.*

Bernard is actually *proud* of these creations.

"The only good thing about Bernard is that my mom's in a better mood since she met him," I told Genevieve on the phone.

"I think it's interesting to have a dating mother," Genevieve replied.

"No it isn't, it's terrible. It's the *last* thing I want. But the worst part is *who* she's dating. I can't believe she likes Bernard. He's totally unsuitable." I was remembering the word my mom used to describe the men all those ex-convicts went out with.

"What's wrong with him?" Genevieve was curious.

"Everything. He's always trying to get me to like him, but it's so fake. And I can't like him. There's something I just can't overlook."

"What?"

"His basic personality."

Genevieve laughed. "For example?"

"He's always writing down everything he eats in a small notebook. He wants to make sure his diet is well-balanced. And he gets on my nerves with his sit-ups and push-ups right before he eats. And he tells us weird stuff."

"What sort of weird stuff?"

"He said he was once followed by a private detective. Why would anyone want people to know something like that? And he said he used to belong to a nudist colony. Gross! And he said he used to be a scuba diver until his best friend had an accident and got paralysed from going up to the surface too fast. He said he used to be in a rock band where everyone except him took heroin, and finally the lead guitarist overdosed and died. And he said he used to drive a motorcycle until one time he sailed off a bridge and had to be rescued by the police."

"Do you think it's all true?" Genevieve asked suspiciously.

"Well, I didn't think so at first, but he brought over slides. Slides of his entire life! His baby pictures, his bar-mitzvah, his first wedding, his second wedding, his son coming out of his second wife, the scuba-diver in a wheelchair, the rock musician's funeral, the bashed-up motorcycle under the bridge. Nothing was left to the imagination, believe me" (illustration 19).

Yesterday I brought a picture of Bernard to show Genevieve. Naturally he gave my mom about fifty pictures of himself, so she could look at him from all angles.

I chose the one of Bernard on a beach in tiny red shorts. He was standing there holding his surfboard and looking like a show-off, a braggart, a swashbuckler, a hollow man, a straw man and a big bag of wind.

"He looks like my Uncle Gaetan," Genevieve remarked when she saw the photo. "My mom says Gaetan is a bum who sponges off women," she added.

"Well, he's certainly not sponging off my mom," I replied. "There's nothing to sponge."

"Speaking of sponging, can you help me with square roots?" Genevieve begged.

She's been trying really hard this year (guess why), and her marks have gone up slightly.

"Are you kidding? I'm practically suicidal because of square roots! We'll both have to ask Leila."

As for Yoshi, we've decided to see each other in secret. In school we act like the other person doesn't even exist, hoping the storm will blow over. But we've been talking on the phone every day and we're trying to figure out where we can meet and not be seen. It isn't easy. Now I know what Romeo and Juliet went through.

Thank God for Genevieve. At least there's one person I can talk to about Yoshi and what's going on. She's in love too, so she knows what it's like.

## 28

Well, things are quietening down *a little* at school. The strategy Yoshi and I are using (ignoring each other in public) is working. I think everyone's beginning to assume that we broke up. Or maybe they just got bored with tormenting me and are now looking for some helpless animals they can do experiments on.

Actually, my relationship with Yoshi is moving in a promising direction. There's still a lot I don't know about him and I wish he'd invite me over to see his place. Why doesn't he want me to visit him? Does he have a vampire living with him, or what?

Genevieve's brother Raymond has been helping me and Genevieve with our opera presentation. I was very surprised. For the first time in his entire life, he didn't break into hysterical laughter at the thought of how he tricked me and Genevieve into believing we had to hide from the bombs of World War Three.

He acted like a normal person, for a change.

First, he found a great costume for Genevieve. His high school put on this musical, *The Pirates of Penzance*, last year, and he dug out one of the pirate costumes. It fits Genevieve perfectly. There's a long, puffy white top with lace cuffs, three-quarter black pants, a leather belt with a buckle, and a vest. Raymond also got us an awesome sword.

Genevieve looks fantastic in this outfit. The only thing missing is a hat, because the pirate's hat isn't right for Edgar, of course. But Raymond says we don't need a hat. He says we should tie Genevieve's hair in a pony-tail with a black velvet ribbon, because that was the style for men back then, and all she needs is a mous-tache, which he offered to draw on the day of the performance (in three days!).

My costume is a long, pale blue satin and lace gown from my Aunt Hilda's wedding. Hilda had it made specially for my mom, and now my mom and Hilda are not on speaking terms because my mom refused to wear the satin bow, and as a result Hilda wouldn't let her be in the wedding photo, and they began fighting about some goldfish from the far and distant past, and now for three years they haven't been on speaking terms. However, the dress is fabulous, and

I like that bow. I don't know what Mom had against it. She can be so stubborn!

The dress didn't have to be shortened, because I'm already taller than my mom by two inches. I guess I take after my father, who's over six feet.

The only problem with the dress was on top, since my mom has sort of big boobs while mine are still trying to decide whether to make an appearance or not. We solved the problem by finding a feathery boa-type scarf which I will drape around my neck and which will cover the loose part of the dress. The boa scarf is bright red and doesn't really go with the pale blue satin, but Mom says it's fine, because opera stars like to stand out. Mom's also going to do my hair up in this really complicated way that she learnt to do when she was in the opera business herself.

Augusta's helping, too. She's going to do my make-up. I had to forgive her for spreading those rumours. It's too stressful to be on bad terms with Augusta. And she did sort of apologize on Instant Messenger:

**hips dont lie and neither do lips** *says:*

*hey i was only joking didnt mean to make a big thing howsit going?*

As for Genevieve, she's been practising falling dead off a chair since Christmas. Raymond gave her some tips on how to make it realistic.

Then, just when we were starting to trust Raymond, just when we were thinking he had turned over a new leaf, he just *had* to go and say, "Hey, Gen, now you'll know how to duck under a chair when the bombs come raining down on Canada."

Genevieve hit him with a skating magazine and he began to pretend that he was wounded from one of the explosions of World War Three.

We left him holding his stomach and moaning "Mother, Mother, come say good-bye!" and we walked over to my dad's place, where it's possible to have some peace and quiet.

## 29

Our presentation of *Lucia de Lammermoor* was today. It was a big hit!

In the morning Mom did my hair up. She did a surprisingly good job, with this special wiry thing that she has from her opera days. Then we went to school a half-hour early with our costumes and the glasses for the squeaky sound, for when Lucia loses her mind. Augusta came early too, to do my make-up. She's been hanging out with Clyve, the guy from Sir John Crimps Academy who was at the party, so we haven't seen that much of her lately. She says that Clyve "has not yet expressed his feelings about the two of us, but I can tell he loves me." Imagine going through life believing that people can't help loving you!

She sat me down at an empty desk, opened a huge box filled with eyeliner and blush and eye shadow and mascara and lipstick, all in about a million colours, and got to work. She was so serious, you'd think she was doing brain surgery. Finally we had to force her to stop, because the bell was about to ring. We made a dash for the bathroom. I put on the gown and Genevieve put on the *Pirates of Penzance* costume.

Everyone began to clap when we got into the classroom, and we hadn't even started.

In fact, we couldn't start right away, because first we had to do a math quiz. It was strange doing a math quiz in high heels and a gown, with my hair done up.

After the quiz, Mr. Pete called us up. At first there was a low hum of tittering and guffaws and throat-clearing from the back of the classroom, and someone said, "She did it her way," but Mr. Pete gave the class a look and everyone got quiet. Mr. Pete's looks are very effective.

I began by telling the class about the history of opera and about Donizetti's life — he's the guy who wrote the opera. It was very sad. In one year his baby died — two had already died — then his wife, who was only 29, died, then his parents died, then his sister died. People died a lot in those days. They didn't have decent plumbing so their hygiene was poor. Then, when they got sick, they didn't have antibiotics. Poor them!

"In the end, he lost his mind, just like Lucia," I disclosed. "He died of a disease like AIDS that people had in those days, and which makes you go crazy."

Then Genevieve and I acted out the story of *Lucia de Lammermoor*. I was supposed to say, "*Were he but here, oh ecstasy, I would know no sorrow!*" But I just couldn't. Not after recent events at school.

So I just said, "I wish Edgar would show up."

That's when I got to go crazy. That was *my* favourite part. I waved my arms like Mrs. Clean does, and I stumbled around and threw pieces of paper in the air (Raymond's idea).

My performance gave me a chance to show my classmates how their recent behaviour has affected me.

The only thing that didn't work was the squeaky glasses. I filled them with water and put them on Mr. Pete's desk and tried to make them squeak, but I couldn't get much sound out of them. At least we got to explain about how the sound drove sopranos up a wall.

Genevieve got up on a chair and passionately recited, "*You have spread your wings to heaven, spirit pure and tender!*" It turned out that Mr. Pete knows that opera! He began to sing that part in Italian! He knew it by heart. No one laughed. On the contrary, everyone clapped. He has a really good voice.

Then Genevieve stabbed herself with the sword. The class was impressed by how realistically she fell down dead. Before she died she even did a few death throes, to make it more horrible.

Mr. Pete came up to both of us, shook our hands and said, "Marvellous presentation. Excellent! Congratulations. Genevieve, you are a born actress." Genevieve almost fainted in my arms.

The problem with performing, I find, is that it's hard to go back to ordinary life.

You want it to last and last, and instead you have to go back to your desk and take out your math book and become an ordinary person again, like all the other ordinary people.

When I become a famous novelist, I'll be able to get attention wherever I go, even in math class.

Btw, my mom is still seeing that Bernard.

## 30

"Yoshi, I have something I want to ask you." (Zane says it's good to start a chapter with a quote, before you tell the story.)

We had finally found a safe place to go to together. We went to see a production of *Phantom of the Opera* put on by Women for People Who Have Less. A few People Who Have Less were going to act in the play and all the money was going to a shelter in Toronto.

We figured we wouldn't run into anyone there because (a) it was in another town and (b) no one knew about it. The only reason I got to hear about the play was because several of my mom's ex-convict clients were helping out.

It was one of our warmest days this year. You could feel in the air that spring's coming soon. Mom gave us a lift. Her car's back from the garage, but the mechanic says it "isn't long for this world." He's in the Ghent Evangelical

Choir, so he has a poetic way of putting things.

As we were driving there, I decided I was going to confront Yoshi about why we never go to his place.

So when we were in the lobby of this tiny theatre, waiting to be let in, I told Yoshi I had to ask him something. There wasn't an immense crowd, as you can imagine.

"What is it?" Yoshi asked nervously.

"How come you never ask me over to your place?"

"How come you never ask me over to your mother's place?" he tried to distract me.

"I told you why." (I did.) "My mom's house is lopsided, run-down and embarrassing."

Yoshi didn't say anything.

"So?"

He coughed and looked at his shoes.

I insisted. "Don't you think if we're going to be friends you have to trust me? Do you have werewolves living with you?"

He nodded.

"Very funny," I said.

"Well, not werewolves, but my ... my family."

"Your family?"

Just then a Man Who Has Less, and who also has the longest and yellowest fingernails I've ever seen in my life, opened the door, so we had to stop talking and take our seats.

The play was pretty bad. Everyone sang off-key, the set fell down twice, the Man Who Has Less (who also played the Phantom) had two coughing fits, and a woman behind us kept saying over and over, "I saw this on *Broadway*." I wanted to strangle her (illustration 20).

At intermission, I urged Yoshi to continue.

He sighed. "Aside from my parents, I live with my great-aunt, my uncle, my great-cousin and my grand-mother," he said gloomily.

"What's a great-cousin?" I asked.

"I have no idea."

"So, what's the problem?"

"Well, they're very old-fashioned," he said darkly. "Especially my older relatives. If I bring you home, they'll just assume that ..." he blushed.

"That I'm your future wife?" I guessed.

"Uh-huh. And I'll never hear the end of it. Have I inspected your family? Do you have an unblemished background? Do you have a dowry? A dowry, for God's sake."

"What's a dowry?" I asked.

"That's money or stuff you bring into the marriage with you," he mumbled.

Poor Yoshi! At least when I was tormented at school I could count on not having my privacy invaded at home. But Yoshi would be getting it from both ends.

"I see your problem," I said. "But couldn't you just explain?"

Yoshi only sighed more deeply.

My mom picked us up after the play was over and then we picked up Bernard and the four of us went out for dinner, except that Yoshi and I sat at a separate table.

I warned my mom that if she gave any indication that she and Bernard are more than business-like acquaintances, I'd move into my dad's for good and she would never, ever see me again.

She said okay, and I admit she kept her promise. Still, it was sort of annoying having her and that crazy Bernard with us. But we had no choice. We're too young to drive.

I've decided that Yoshi is definitely my type.

## 31

Very, very good news.

Mr. Pete gave us an assignment called "Facts and Opinions." We were supposed to choose a topic, collect the facts, and then give our opinion, based on the facts.

Mr. Pete wrote out a long list of topics to choose from. I chose plastic surgery, which turned out to be an excellent topic because, amazingly, it led to the disappearance of Bernard from our lives.

I came home from school and first I did all the fact-searching, the way Mr. Pete told us to do it. He taught us how to tell the difference between good and bad sites on the internet. Good sites are from universities or famous newspapers or famous scientists. Bad sites are from someone you don't know, who could be a ten-year-old kid, or corporations with Vested Interests, like beef farmers setting up websites about how soy can kill you.

Meanwhile, Bernard came to visit. He was having coffee and health donuts at the kitchen table with my mom.

So I decided to see whether Bernard and Mom could help me get some ideas for the Opinion part of my assignment.

It turned out that Mom and Bernard didn't exactly agree.

At first they were polite and calm. Mom said that the plastic surgery craze is a symptom of a sexist, lookist society, and that it's in partnership with the Fashion Industry's attempt to make women and girls insecure and unhappy so they'll spend more money. She also said that only shallow, stupid men want a woman who looks like a plastic Barbie. Finally she said that it was too bad women were being "sucked into trying to fit into some adolescent male fantasy of what a woman should look like," and that women like that would never be happy, because the men they were trying to please would never be satisfied — they were too immature.

Bernard had a different point of view.

He said love of beauty was a natural human instinct. He said famous paintings proved that.

He said my mom would look better and feel better

if she dyed her hair to get rid of the grey streaks.

"You can just forget it," Mom said in a hostile voice. "If you think I'm going to dye my hair to please you, you're out of your mind, Bernard."

Some more unpleasant things were said. By then I was back in my room with the door closed, but it wasn't hard to hear what my mom was saying. Basically, my mom told Bernard he was egoistical, self-centered, self-obsessed, self-serving, self-loving, self-absorbed and a creep — and she didn't even use a thesaurus. I'm impressed.

Bernard murmured something I didn't hear, and left.

I felt it was safe to emerge from my room at that point. "I guess Bernard's not your boyfriend any more," I said, trying to hide my joy.

"That's right," Mom said curtly.

Then she added, "When you grow up and have a boyfriend, Pauline, just make sure he doesn't spend half an hour admiring himself in the mirror every morning."

I could have told *her* that.

Then she ate seventeen health donuts. She's going to feel sick. I feel sick just thinking about it.

Anyway, I took a lot of notes while Mom was talking, and I wrote a really detailed Opinion. Mr. Pete will be impressed.

Gotta get to square roots now. Help!

## 32

I have lost my best friend.

I had a best friend, but that part of my life has ended.

Yes, Genevieve, my true and loyal friend for nine years, has betrayed, forsaken, abandoned and defrauded me.

"Listen," she casually mentioned last week, "I'm not coming to school for the next few days. I have to get into shape and then compete."

"When? Where? I'm coming!"

"Oh, don't bother, Pauline. It's so far away, it's a five-hour drive. And it's so long and boring. I'll do my whole routine for you in private, I promise."

"Forget it. I wouldn't miss this for anything."

My dad agreed to drive me. We took Mom's car instead of the pick-up to save on gas.

It wasn't a five-hour drive, it was only a three-hour drive. But it felt like five hours. I *was* rather bored.

However, I didn't ask *When are we going to get there?* even once. It took incredible self-control.

The weather was not great either. It got very cold again this week.

But once we were there, it was really exciting. The arena was packed. And then I noticed TV cameras down below. For some reason, when I saw those cameras, I felt awful! I began to sweat and I felt like throwing up. I was so nervous for Genevieve, exactly as if I was the one skating.

My dad found out that Genevieve had skated her short program the day before, and she'd come in first, which didn't surprise me. Now she had to do the long program.

There were four skaters before her. They were really good. And their costumes were beautiful too. But three of them fell once, and the fourth skater fell about five times. The first time a skater fell, I almost jumped out of my seat. I felt so bad for her! But Dad reminded me that even Olympic champions fall.

No wonder! How can you leap up in the air and then land on what is basically a blade the width of *cardboard* without falling?

Finally Genevieve came on. Her costume was stunning! Very pale pink with tiny diamonds sprinkled around her neckline and along the sleeves. She looked like a fairy on ice.

I was too nervous to really pay attention to her skating. I just kept praying she wouldn't fall. I was clutching my seat and I felt sick.

And she didn't fall. The audience kept cheering and clapping so I figured she was doing very well. When she was finished, she had really high points.

I was starving by then, so my dad suggested we leave, grab a bite, then come back when it was over. He was pretty exhausted, I think. So that's what we did. We found a bakery and we bought some very tasty salads and rolls and date squares, which we ate in the car with chocolate milk. I spilled some chocolate milk on the seat, I hope Mom won't mind. She can be a little fanatic about things like that.

When we came back we saw right away that Genevieve had won. It was up there on the score-board, her name on top in big letters, GENEVIEVE BINETTE, and then the other skaters underneath.

We had to push through tons of people to get to her. My dad's tall, so he got us through the mob. Mostly the mob consisted of Genevieve's relatives. They're a very big family.

Genevieve was standing near the dressing room,

and there was a TV crew there. She was being interviewed for television. I couldn't hear what she said, but
she looked as happy as she did when we brought her
that get-well card from Mr. Pete.

After that, her father was interviewed. By then we
were closer, so I heard him. From the way he talked,
you'd think *he'd* won the gold medal. "We worked
hard, we put a lot into it, we struggled, and it's paid
off," he said. Maybe he was referring to the money.

Finally the interviews were over, the TV people left,
and the crowd began to clear. I went over to give
Genevieve a congratulations hug. To my surprise, she
looked really depressed when she saw me.

Then I noticed that standing right next to her was
this other girl, around our age, who was giving me this
really cold stare. She had gold-red hair and perfect but
boring features, like someone in a magazine ad for hair
dye or insurance.

"Genevieve, you were fantastic!" I exclaimed. "I was
so excited I couldn't breathe, watching you. I could
barely look."

The girl with the gold-red hair was still staring at
me. She was cramping my style.

My dad said, "Congratulations."

Genevieve mumbled, "Thanks." She looked miserable.

"I'm Pauline, by the way," I said, making a super-human effort to be friendly.

"Pauline, Morgan," Genevieve muttered.

"Hi Pauline-by-the-way," Morgan said imperiously. She was trying to be mean, but it didn't work. "I'm Genevieve's best friend," Morgan continued. "I'm her good luck charm when she skates and she's mine at swimming, and one day we're going to go to the Olympics together. We're inseparable!"

I figured Morgan was one of those people who like to pretend they know famous people. A stalker type. I hoped there was good security in the arena.

"Isn't that true, Gen?" Morgan continued.

To my astonishment, Genevieve nodded!

But I still thought it was some kind of mistake. Maybe the girl was a sad, unwell person and Genevieve didn't want to offend her, in case she hadn't taken her meds. I decided to ignore her. I said, "So, let's go out to celebrate! What are your plans?"

Morgan answered immediately. "Oh, we booked a table at the hotel ages ago. Sorry, there's no room for any more. It's only for close friends. Right, Gen?"

Genevieve *hates* when people call her Gen. That alone proved the girl was lying. But Genevieve nodded again! She mumbled something I couldn't hear, but which had the words "sorry" and "wish" and "can't" in it.

For a moment I just stood there, stunned, stupefied, dazed and spaced out.

Then I said, "I have to go." And I turned and walked away.

My dad didn't say anything. He knew what was going on, believe me. He doesn't miss much. But he probably couldn't think what to say.

We drove home in silence. My mom would be talking about what happened the whole way home, but not my dad.

Finally, I blurted out, "I'm sorry I ever went! I'm never talking to her again! I wasted my whole day, and I hate this long, boring drive."

My dad said, "Do you want to stop for ice cream?" Ice cream, at a time like this! Does he think I'm a child!? Still, I guess he was doing his best. But I was in a mean mood, so I just said, "No, thanks," in this really cold voice.

The next day at school there was a big crowd around Genevieve. As soon as she saw me she waved and called out "Hi," as though nothing had happened.

"Go away and don't ever come back!" I cried out, even though where could she go? We're in the same class and we hang around with the same kids.

"But ..." She looked very surprised.

"I hate you!" I screamed. The words just came out. I didn't know I was going to say them, or even that I felt that way. I ran off.

I haven't talked to Genevieve for three days now. We're divorced.

I'm in a bad mood. I feel broody and overcome with existential ennui. That means feeling restless because life is meaningless. Mr. Pete taught us that expression (illustration 21).

My mom brought home a bald man with a big stomach named Laurie. So what if it's a girl's name? Who cares? It's not my problem.

She asked me first, of course. "Okay if I invite an old friend for supper?"

"Oh, who cares," I grunted.

"We studied singing together. He was a baritone," she went on.

"How interesting," I replied sardonically.

"Come on, Pauline, cheer up," she said encouragingly.

"Look who's talking!" I shouted angrily and stomped to my room. I would have slammed the door, but it's broken like everything else in this dump, and it comes off its hinges if you slam it.

During supper I tried to ignore Laurie, but I found out a few things anyway. He used to study opera like my mom, but he left to join a Buddhist cult. They didn't believe in opera, only in chanting. Then when he left the cult, it was too late to go back to singing. He'd lost his voice from all the chanting.

I got up in the middle of the meal, mumbled an excuse and went to my room. I thought, *If you want to make a fool of yourself, Mom, go right ahead, but I don't have to watch.*

I couldn't even tell Genevieve about this latest development in my mom's life. Twice she left notes in my desk. Once she wrote, *Let's talk* and another time, *I'm sorry.* I ignored both notes.

I tried to tell Yoshi what had happened, but I could see he didn't understand. It's not his fault. Boys don't really have friends, have you noticed? They just *do* things together. I mean, have you ever heard a guy in your class tell another guy, "I'm never talking to you again, you lied to me and double-crossed me"? Neither have I. It's probably genetic.

I've stopped doing my homework. I bring magazines to school and read them right under Mr. Pete's eyes.

Art and PE I've been skipping altogether. And in French I stare out the window and let the meaningless words drift right by me.

When Mr. Pete asks me for my homework, I say in a voice full of existential ennui, "I don't have it."

He sighs and says, "La vie, la vie," which means "Life, Life" but which really means: Life can be a real pain.

Finally, today, he asked me to stay in at lunchtime to talk to him.

"So, Pauline, what's going on?" he asked with a worried look.

"Nothing," I replied in a voice you could barely hear.

"My best friend is dying of AIDS," he said suddenly. I just stared at him. "Yes, it's true, he is. And any day now he's going to go. But look, I have no choice, I have to go to work, teach — my students count on me."

"Well, no one's counting on me, so it doesn't matter," I replied. Then, without knowing I was going to say it, just like with Genevieve, I blurted out, "What do I care about your stupid friend anyway?" Then I ran to the bathroom and locked myself in a stall and cried.

I felt so bad about what I had said that I couldn't go back to class. I went to the mall instead and looked at T-shirts.

## 34

Mr. Pete called my dad at home, and they talked for about an hour. My dad laughed a few times, so I figured it couldn't be too bad.

"That was Pete Lester," Dad said when he got off the phone. "He says you're in a bad mood these days. Still upset about Genevieve?"

"I'm fine! Just leave me alone!" I went to my room and slammed the door and stared at Mrs. Clean. She was eating oranges for a change. I guess the supermarket ran out of grapes.

My dad knocked on the door and came in. He sat down at my desk. Only he didn't say anything. That's what my mom always used to complain about, that he didn't say anything. I went on staring at Mrs. Clean.

Finally, he said something. He said, "What do you want for supper?"

"Anything," I mumbled.

"Spaghetti okay?"

"Yeah."

So he went to the kitchen and made us spaghetti.

"Mom has a new boyfriend," I said scathingly while we were eating. "His name is Laurie, a girl's name. He's bald and fat and he used to be a baritone but he joined a cult."

"Laurie Levy?" my dad smiled. "I know him. Did he go bald?"

"Pretty bald."

"He's a nice guy. Mom and I used to play Trivial Pursuit with him and his wife. What was her name?" he tried to remember. "Annette, that's right."

"Was that before or after the cult?" I asked sarcastically.

"After. It wasn't really a cult, you know. Just a Buddhist lifestyle. I think he got bored with it. But he met Annette there, so at least he got something out of it."

"Well, they're divorced now, otherwise why didn't Annette come with him to Mom's?"

Too bad my dad thinks Laurie's nice. I don't want him to be nice.

My dad must have talked to my mom, because she phoned me and said, "I won't invite Laurie again, Pauline.

He just called me up suddenly, you know. He said he
needed to talk to someone so I invited him over."

"Why wasn't he with his wife?"

"Annette left him. That's why he wanted to talk."

"Is he going to be your boyfriend?" I asked in a
rude voice.

"I don't know," Mom replied, which means YES.

Yoshi called, but it was only a short call, to say that
he was going out to play soccer with some friends, and
he'd call again tomorrow. I think pretending during
the day that we don't know the other person exists is
putting a strain on our relationship.

Or maybe it's just my mood.

Should I give Genevieve a second chance? For one
thing, I never really gave her a chance to explain. Maybe
there's a good reason why she lied to me for several
years. Like maybe the red-haired girl is really some sort
of evil alien in disguise who's blackmailing Genevieve.

Or something.

I don't know. I'll think about it. I'm undecided,
ambivalent, infirm of purpose and at sea.

## 35

I went up to Genevieve today during lunch recess. "All right, explain," I said in a leaden, impassive voice.

"I'm sorry," she said, staring at her yoghurt.

The thing is, "I'm sorry" doesn't always work. Like for example, there was this story in the paper about a couple who left a teenager in charge of their dog when they went on vacation and when they came back, the teenager had accidentally burned down the house and the dog was missing. Somehow, you get the feeling that "I'm sorry" just wouldn't work in a case like that.

I didn't say anything. I just stood over her with folded arms. Rachel and Leila weren't around; they've been sort of avoiding us. I guess they don't want to get involved.

"I knew you'd hate her," Genevieve went on. "I mean, I knew *why* you'd hate her. I mean ..." She looked so confused I started feeling a bit sorry for her.

I sat down opposite her. "I can't believe it. I can't believe you've had a *secret* friend all this time, that you didn't tell me about!"

"She's Bruno's daughter," Genevieve said. Bruno is her skating coach, the one who used to be famous when he was young and thin.

Genevieve really was looking pitiful. She was starting to remind me of Stormy Weather when she's waiting for her Kitty Treats.

"I couldn't *not* be nice to her. Bruno kept bringing us together, because Morgan doesn't have that many friends."

"I wonder why that is," I said bitterly.

"Well ... she's different once you get to know her. But I knew you'd hate her. It's just that ... I don't know. Her mother is really mean to her, pushing her like crazy and yelling at her if she doesn't come first every time. Swimming is her whole life, and the only reason she likes me is that she thinks I'm like her. That I'm as crazy about skating as she is about swimming, and she thinks I'm the only person who can understand her. And maybe I am."

"But why didn't you *tell* me?"

"Because you'd want to meet her, and I knew it would be a disaster."

"So you've been leading a double life," I said accusingly.

"I *do* lead a double life. I mean, I want to be normal, but I also want to be a top skater. But you're my best friend. I hardly even ever see Morgan, and I see you every day, and you're the one who knows everything about me."

"But she said *she* was your best friend! And you agreed with her!"

"What could I do?" Genevieve looked at me helplessly. "I didn't want to hurt her feelings. I'm like all she has, apart from her swimming. She only said that because she's always scared I'll stop liking her."

Genevieve was actually sort of crying by now. She doesn't cry easily, but her eyes were getting red and watery, and the tip of her nose was also getting red. For Genevieve, that's hysterics.

"When do you see her?"

"She comes to see me practise sometimes, and then we go for a health-shake. And I try to get to her tournaments when I can. And we talk on the phone sometimes."

"It's just so weird. I feel like you kept a big part of your life a secret. Like you don't trust me."

"I do trust you. I trust you more than anyone else —

I mean, along with my parents. And of course Pete …"
She sighed, then went on. "But I can't discuss my injuries
and my diet and the other competitors with you, and
what it's like to have people judging you all the time.
I don't *want* to talk to you about all that. You'd get
bored, and besides, I like getting a break from skating.
That's where I'm completely different from Morgan.
She never takes a break. I'd die if I lived like that."

"Oh …" I said vaguely.

"You know, Morgan really might make it to the
Olympics. I'm sure I'll get better and better, but I
really don't think I'll ever go that far. I think you have
to be like Morgan to go that far. Skating's important
for me, but not, you know … not at the expense of
everything else. One skater I read about got so stressed
at one point that her hair started falling out!"

I didn't say anything. I was digesting what she was
saying.

"Anyway, I really am sorry," Genevieve said.

Suddenly I didn't even know what she should be
sorry about. So she had another friend, so what? Morgan
sounded kind of pathetic. Why shouldn't Genevieve be
her friend?

And why shouldn't she be allowed to have her own
private life?

It's just that she should have trusted me. Why didn't she tell me? I would have understood. All she had to do was say, *I know this really weird kid who's into swimming and I have to be her friend because she's my coach's daughter.*

But that would be disloyal to Morgan.

Maybe what I was seeing was actually one of the things I like most about Genevieve. She didn't want to talk about Morgan behind her back. But why couldn't I join them for the celebration dinner, after I drove all that way?

"Why didn't you let me come with you to celebrate?" I asked. "And what's this *Gen* business!?"

"I didn't think you were really going to show up, Pauline, so we didn't plan for you. And there really wasn't any more room, we only reserved one table at the restaurant and my parents were already wondering how they'd squeeze us all in, with all my relatives and everything. And it would have been boring for you, we wouldn't have been able to talk or anything."

Now that she'd explained what happened, I felt like a total fool. "I'm sorry too," I said. "I should have talked it over with you."

"It's okay," Genevieve smiled. "Will you come to my birthday party?"

"Of course I'm coming. Congratulations about winning, by the way," I added.

Her smile got wider. "Thanks. I still can't believe it!"

She looked around to make sure no one was listening, then she lowered her voice and said, "Do you think Pete was impressed? I was thinking of him when I went on the ice."

"I'm sure he was impressed. I'll bet he loves figure skating. And listen, I have something to tell you." I was so glad I could finally talk to her. "My mom has a new boyfriend. His name is Laurie!"

We laughed. I admit it was a relief to have a best friend again.

"Listen," she said, "I have news too, though it's not as interesting as yours. I have a math tutor. Her name's Aisha. You can come with me if you want." Genevieve knows I've fallen way behind. Everyone in the class knows. Every day Mr. Pete looks at me and says, "Pauline, Pauline, how are you ever going to catch up?"

So I went with Genevieve to the math tutor. She's a university student and she's studying Chemistry. She showed us a picture of her boyfriend. He's so cute! He's already in pre-med because he's going to be a doctor.

Why can't my mom have a boyfriend like that?

## 36

Yesterday was Genevieve's birthday party. I'm the only person not related to the family who gets invited, because there's no room left for more friends, once all the relatives come. There were cousins, aunts, great-aunts, second cousins, second cousins once removed, third cousins twice removed, a hundred uncles, many old people, and six dogs.

Cake got thrown on the floor by babies, peanuts got thrown in the air by teenagers, juice got spilled by adults, and Genevieve was told she was making her parents proud about six thousand times. There was nowhere to escape to. Every corner of the house was being used up.

I came home to a very contrasting scene. My mom was sitting on the sofa, crying and eating lemon meringue pie.

When she saw me she pretended she wasn't crying.

"What happened?" I asked right away.

"Nothing," she answered.

"Is Laurie coming over?"

"No. His wife decided to go back to him."

"Oh … Well, Genevieve's party was wild as usual. I ate so much cake I think I'm going to throw up."

"That's nice," Mom said. I assumed she meant about the cake, not about throwing up.

Since hearing about happy people wasn't helping Mom feel better, I decided to try talking about miserable people. Maybe that would make Mom perk up, seeing as her situation wasn't as bad as theirs.

"Mr. Pete's friend is dying of AIDS," I informed her.

"That's nice," Mom said again. This time I knew for a fact she wasn't listening.

"Mom, did you hear what I said?"

"Oh, sorry, I was … just wondering what to make for supper."

I went to do my homework, but Mom called Dad and said, "Could you please take Pauline tonight? I don't feel too great."

We put on our jackets and walked over to my dad's house. On the way there, she said, "You know what, Pauline? I'm going to go away for a vacation. I haven't had one in a long time. They owe me two weeks at work, and I need to go somewhere peaceful."

"Okay," I said, though I felt a bit weird. I don't know why, except that my mom wasn't her usual self. When I was a kid I used to worry that my parents had been kidnapped and replaced by doubles who just looked like them but were actually operated by evil extraterrestrials. It's not the most pleasant feeling. I mean I knew it was my mother talking about a vacation, not a replacement, but I hated the feeling of her being different.

Today when I came home from school, my dad said, "Mom's gone to Mexico."

"That was fast. Couldn't she wait to say good-bye?" I felt really insulted.

"There was an early flight she wanted to catch. Don't worry, she said she'll phone as soon as she gets there, and e-mail us every day."

My mom did call at around ten, but we could hardly hear her because the connection was so bad. She said the hotel is a bit more run-down than she expected and there's no hot water and the phones don't work too well. "But the beach is beautiful," she yelled into the phone. Then the line went dead.

It's okay. I'm getting used to my life being unpredictable, erratic and amorphous.

Someone should write an opera about me.

## 37

A very weird thing happened, which led to a lot of other stuff.

Rachel came home with me after school and as soon as we opened the door, my dad said, "I have some bad news. The lady next door passed away." He meant Mrs. Clean.

"Oh," I said blankly. I wondered why he looked so sad.

"That's too bad," Rachel said politely. She didn't know who Mrs. Clean was.

"How did she die?" I asked curiously.

"Well, that's the sad part. I'm afraid she took her own life."

"You mean killed herself?" Rachel sounded very shocked.

"Yes," Dad nodded.

"Oh, that's terrible!" Rachel said feelingly. "That's awful."

"How did she do it?" I asked.

"I think she swallowed poison or sleeping pills," Dad replied sadly. Why was he so upset, I wondered. He always used to say she was "a real case."

Rachel and I went to my bedroom and looked out the window into Mrs. Clean's kitchen.

Her box of shells was right on the kitchen table. Suddenly, I felt that Mrs. Clean put that box there for me. I can't explain, but I was sure of it.

"Rachel, I have to go out for a second, okay?"

"Sure," Rachel said.

I went out back, climbed over the fence to Mrs. Clean's backyard, and tried her back door. It wasn't locked. I snuck quickly into the house, grabbed the box, and brought it back with me.

The box is very old. It's made of metal with gold designs, except that most of the gold's peeled off. There's a faded picture of a boy in an orange velvet jacket with lace at the collar and at the sleeves, and he's sitting on something that's either a rock or a sofa. It's hard to tell because the picture is so faded. I'll try to draw the boy for you (illustration 22). The box was probably really pretty once.

"What's that?" Rachel asked.

"The woman who died used to polish these shells,"

I replied. "I think she'd want someone to look after them. She had two foster children, you know. I wonder whether they know what happened. What if no one tells them?" When I said that I began to cry a little, and that made Rachel cry, too.

I thought of Lucia de Lammermoor and how she died for love, but I couldn't imagine anyone loving Mrs. Clean, with her old clothes and strange habits and the hair on her chin. She never even had visitors.

Probably even her foster children didn't love her, because they were only foster children and one of them was wild.

Suddenly I felt very wild myself.

I went over to my dad and shouted at the top of my lungs, "It's your fault! It's all your fault. You made fun of Mrs. Clean! And if Mom never comes back it'll be your fault too. You're the worst father in the world! I never want to see you again!"

And I ran out of the house.

All this in front of Rachel — can you imagine? Rachel of all people! She must have been completely horrified. She's not even allowed to say "darn" to her grandmother.

I ran to Mom's house and got the key from under the mat and let myself in. It was freezing in there, so I turned the heat way up, put on my mom's parka and sat huddled on the sofa.

Words are just flying out of my mouth lately. I say things I don't even know I'm going to say. But usually, what I say turns out to be what I'm really feeling.

I guess my dad took Rachel home. Eventually, the door opened and of course it was him.

As soon as he came in, I went over to the CD player and put on this piece of music I know he hates. It's one of the things my mom said made her glad to be on her own at first. She said she could finally play requiems and masses. My dad doesn't like that sort of music. He says it's too "intrusive."

So I put on this requiem thing by Mozart, which is one of my mom's favourites. I put it on really really loud. Too loud even for me, but I didn't care.

My dad sat on a chair near the TV and didn't say anything.

Finally I mumbled, "What if Mom never comes back from Mexico?" Of course he couldn't hear me because the music was so loud. So he reached over and lowered the volume.

"I didn't hear you," he said calmly.

"What if Mom never comes back from Mexico," I said very loudly. "What if she feels about you the way

Lucia felt about Edgar or Edgar about Lucia? It'll all be your fault! She doesn't care about Griswold or Bernard or Laurie because they're all losers! You're the one she's sad about and it's all your fault because you never talked to her! You never talk to anyone!"

Well, my dad actually answered. For once, he began telling me what was on his mind.

"I know the divorce was harder on Mom than on me," he admitted. "I'm more of a loner. I have you, and I have my painting, and that's enough for me. That's just the way I am. I like peace and quiet. But you know, I do get worried and sad and upset sometimes. I'm just not good at showing my feelings. I prefer to paint when I have something bothering me."

I didn't answer. This was actually quite interesting, so I waited, in case there was more coming. There was.

"As for Mom not coming back from Mexico, that's just ridiculous. Mom loves you. She used to take you out of daycare an hour early every day because she missed you, and she hasn't changed, in case you haven't noticed. And she doesn't do impulsive things. She's about the most responsible person I know. But she's the opposite of me when it comes to telling you what's on her mind," Dad went on. "Whatever she's feeling, she lets you know. She would have made a superb opera singer.

I tried to persuade her not to quit, but she said the life of an opera singer was too hard. That's typical of Barbara. She's so practical."

I felt a bit less angry, but I didn't want to show it. It's embarrassing if you feel less angry too fast, after you've really made a point of being mad.

"I'm sure you could see that the woman next door was different from most people," Dad continued. "Most people figure out a way to solve their problems. No matter how big their problems are, they find a way. Or else they learn to live with them. It's the exception for a person to give up altogether. Listen, if every adult with a problem committed suicide, there'd be very few people left on this planet."

Finally, I said, in a sort of grouchy way, "I don't like when you don't tell me what's going on, and I don't like when Mom *does* tell me what's going on, I mean with her stupid boyfriends, they make me puke!"

He laughed. "You're right," he agreed. "Knowing too much is hard, and not knowing enough is hard. Too bad for all of us! But look at the bright side. If you didn't know anything, you'd feel scared all the time. And if you always saw and knew everything, you'd be pulling the covers over your head!"

"I guess," I mumbled. I wasn't at all mad any more, but I still didn't want to say so.

"Are you hungry?" Dad asked, getting up from the floor and smiling at me.

"Yeah," I admitted.

"How about going to the mall?" he suggested.

"I want to go to La Bohème," I said. Suddenly I really wanted to go there. Maybe my mom's spoiled me by taking me to La Bohème every time there's a big crisis.

"La Bohème! I may have to rob a bank first."

"Please," I begged.

"Okay," he gave in. He always gives in to me.

I'm fairly satisfied with my dad's attempt at communication. For a beginner, he didn't do too badly.

38

I think this is going to be my last chapter.

First of all, this book has to end sometime!

Secondly, today was the last day of school, which I think is a good place to end, because I began this book exactly a year ago. I had no idea it was going to be so much work! Zane Burbank was definitely right about that.

And third, today everything went smoothly for once. So if I stop now, before any new disaster takes place, my novel will have a happy ending. Which is what Zane recommends.

At first I couldn't decide what to call this book. I thought I'd call it *The Truly True Story of a Girl*. I like the *Truly True* part because I've decided that revealing hidden truths isn't as simple as Zane makes it out to be. What's the truth, anyway? Everyone knows some things, but not other things. All people reveal some part of themselves, but not other parts. When is it good to keep things to yourself? When is it bad? I'm going to have to think more about this, some time when I have nothing else to do.

But I decided against that title, because Zane says a title has to be catchy. He says it has to make the book sound *thrilling, gripping and mysterious* so that people will want to read it. So I've decided to call this novel *The Thrilling Life of Pauline de Lammermoor*. That's my pen name, Pauline de Lammermoor. I love that last name. It's very exotic.

I hope this title is catchy enough. I wish I could ask Zane, but he doesn't have a website with a contact number.

Mr. Pete wasn't in school for the last day. He hasn't been in school all week because his best friend died. The whole class sent him a sympathy note, but I sent a separate letter. I had to do that, because of what I'd said to him about his friend.

I wrote:

*Dear Mr. Pete,*

*I'll never forget you as long as I live. You were the best teacher I will ever have. I feel very bad about your friend. I know what it's like to think your best friend doesn't like you any more. It must be a million zillion times worse when your best friend leaves forever, while you're still friends. If he was as nice as you, everyone will miss him for the rest of their lives.*

*Sincerely,*
*Pauline.*

I hope he forgives me for being so insensitive when he first told me about his friend. I mean, I know he will, but will I forgive myself? That must have really hurt him. But on the other hand, Pete understands people. He knows we don't always mean what we say, exactly.

I forgot to tell you, Genevieve passed! By the skin of her teeth, but so what.

Actually, I didn't do that well either, apart from English. I haven't shown my report printout to Mom and Dad yet. Why ruin their mood?

When we were dismissed, me and Genevieve and Rachel and Yoshi all walked over to my dad's to celebrate the fact that we made it through another year of school. My mom came too. She still has her tan from Mexico, though it's faded a bit. She brought me back a beautiful carved box, btw, and I'm keeping Mrs. Clean's shells in it.

Mom baked us a huge three-layer cake with the words, *Congratulations G, P, R & Y!* She didn't have room to spell out all our names.

Yoshi took me aside. "I have something for you."

I noticed before that he was carrying a plastic bag, but I figured it was left-over junk from his locker. I was wrong. He reached into the bag and took out a package wrapped in plain brown paper, which he handed to me. I knew right away it was a painting.

"Thanks!"

"I don't know if you'll like it," Yoshi said modestly, but I had the feeling he was fairly sure I would.

I opened it. By now my parents and Genevieve and Rachel were looking on too.

"OH, NO!" I shrieked.

It was a portrait of me! It even looked like me! Except that I had antennas!

Everyone commented enthusiastically and told Yoshi he was very talented. "Thanks," I said happily. "I love it. This is the coolest gift I ever got in my life. Only why do I have antennas? Am I a Martian? Am I weird?"

"No," Yoshi said. "You're definitely not a Martian. Or weird."

"Then what?"

"You figure it out," he smiled secretively.

"Oh, I almost forgot," Genevieve said. "The secretary gave me an envelope from Pete. It's addressed to both of us."

She took an envelope out of her jacket pocket. It was a bit crinkled from being squished up in her pocket. She tore the envelope open, and inside were two tickets for an opera. From Mr. Pete, of course. He wrote: *This opera by Wolfgang Amadeus Mozart is not quite as tragic as* Lucia de Lammermoor. *I have two tickets I can't use and I thought of you. All the best, Pete Lester.*

The tickets are for an opera in Toronto called *Don Giovanni.*

"Maybe I'll join you, if I may," Mom said.

"Sure, and Yoshi, can you come too?" I asked him.

"Thanks for asking," Yoshi replied. "But I think I'll pass."

"You can have my ticket, Ms. Bloom," Genevieve said politely. "I won't have time to go."

"Opera's not for everyone," Mom said. "But I have a feeling Pauline will like it."

I realized at that moment that I had never actually heard my mom sing opera. So I asked her, "Could you sing a bit of *Lucia de Lammermoor* for us? Please?"

"Oh, I don't know." My mom looked a little shy, but also flattered. "I'm out of shape. I can only fake it at this point."

"Oh, please, Mom," I pleaded.

"Okay, I'll do my best." She went to the laundry room and dug around in her cardboard boxes until she found the right opera score. Then she came back to the living room and sang the part where Lucia begins to rave. She tore at her hair and fell to her knees. She did it in a funny way, though, and everyone laughed.

So now there are only three questions I'm wondering about.

1. Why did Yoshi draw me with antennas?
2. What will grade eight be like?
3. Is my mom's next boyfriend going to be called Wolfgang or Giovanni?

☺

This is where I live when I'm with my Dad

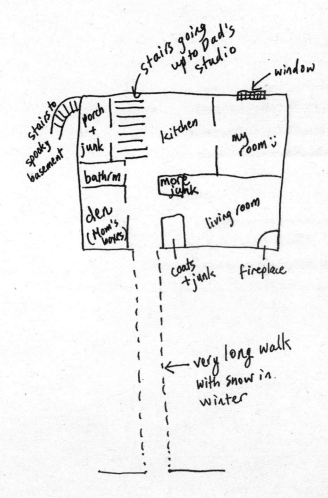

stairs going up to Dad's studio

window

stairs to spooky basement

porch + junk

kitchen

my room ☺

bathrm

more junk

den (Mom's books)

living room

coats + junk

fireplace

← very long walk with snow in winter

Here's a sneak peek at
# Pauline, btw
## BOOK TWO:

Hi! This is me, Pauline Carelli-Bloom, teen author. Two months ago exactly I finished my first novel, which I decided to call *The Thrilling Life of Pauline de Lammermoor.*

I could not have written that novel without the help of Zane Burbank III, who guided me through the trials and tribulations of novel writing with his groundbreaking book, *You Too Can Write a Great Novel!*

It took an entire year to write my first novel. Zane warns authors: *Be prepared to work hard,* and he's not kidding!

I wasn't going to write another novel, but so much has happened in my life that I have no choice but to pick up my pen once again. That's a metaphor, btw, because I actually type on a keyboard like everyone else.

In short, I have to write another novel because if I don't, I'll be "hurled headlong flaming from the ethereal sky, with hideous ruin and combustion, down to bottomless perdition" (John Milton).

In two weeks I'll be starting grade eight in a new school. We're all going to be in a new building — a high school. Our old school, Newton, was shut down due to mould. I thought mould was harmless as long as you didn't eat it, but the government decided that mould is a major health hazard and they shut down the school. Please don't think that all the buildings in this town are either mouldy or being invaded by carpenter ants. Ghent is a very ordinary Ontario town with a mall and quite a few very good restaurants. It's not in a state of decay, it's not spooky, and we don't have any poltergeists.

Anyhow, the entire eighth grade is going to be moved to Pierre Elliot Trudeau High School, because there isn't room for us in any of the middle or elementary schools. There's only room for grade seven in one of them.

Even though I'll know almost everyone, I'm not looking forward to the school year. Your life has to be somewhat stable before you start school, and mine is extremely *un*stable at the moment. In fact, if things go on as they are, I'll probably turn into a drop-out, like most of the women in the halfway house where my mother works. I might even end up with a tattoo.

Zane Burbank III says: *Keep chapters short!* So that's it for now, plus Yoshi is coming over in five minutes. You'll have to wait until the next chapter to find out more!

**The Mysterious Adventures of Pauline Bovary**
is coming soon to bookstores and
libraries near you.

Edeet Ravel was born on an Israeli kibbutz and grew up in Montreal. She is the author of four award-winning novels, including *Ten Thousand Lovers*, which was a finalist for the Governor General's Award, and *A Wall of Light*, winner of the Canadian Jewish Book Award and a finalist for the Giller Prize and Canada/Caribbean Commonwealth Prize. Edeet also works as a peace activist and was a teacher for two decades. She lives in Guelph with her daughter Larissa.

By printing

# The Thrilling Life of
# Pauline
## de Lammermoor

on paper made from 100% post-consumer recycled fibre rather than virgin tree fibre, Raincoast Books has made the following ecological savings:

- 341 trees
- 32,432 kilograms of greenhouse gases (equivalent to driving an average North American car for six years)
- 272 million BTUs (equivalent to the power consumption of a North American home for three years)
- 198,703 litres of water (equivalent to nearly one Olympic sized pool)
- 12,141 kilograms of solid waste (equivalent to nearly one garbage truck load)

(Environmental impact estimates were made using the Environmental Defense Paper Calculator. For more information, visit http://www.papercalculator.org.)